Favorite Children's Stories

from

CHINA and TIBET

W9-DEU-230

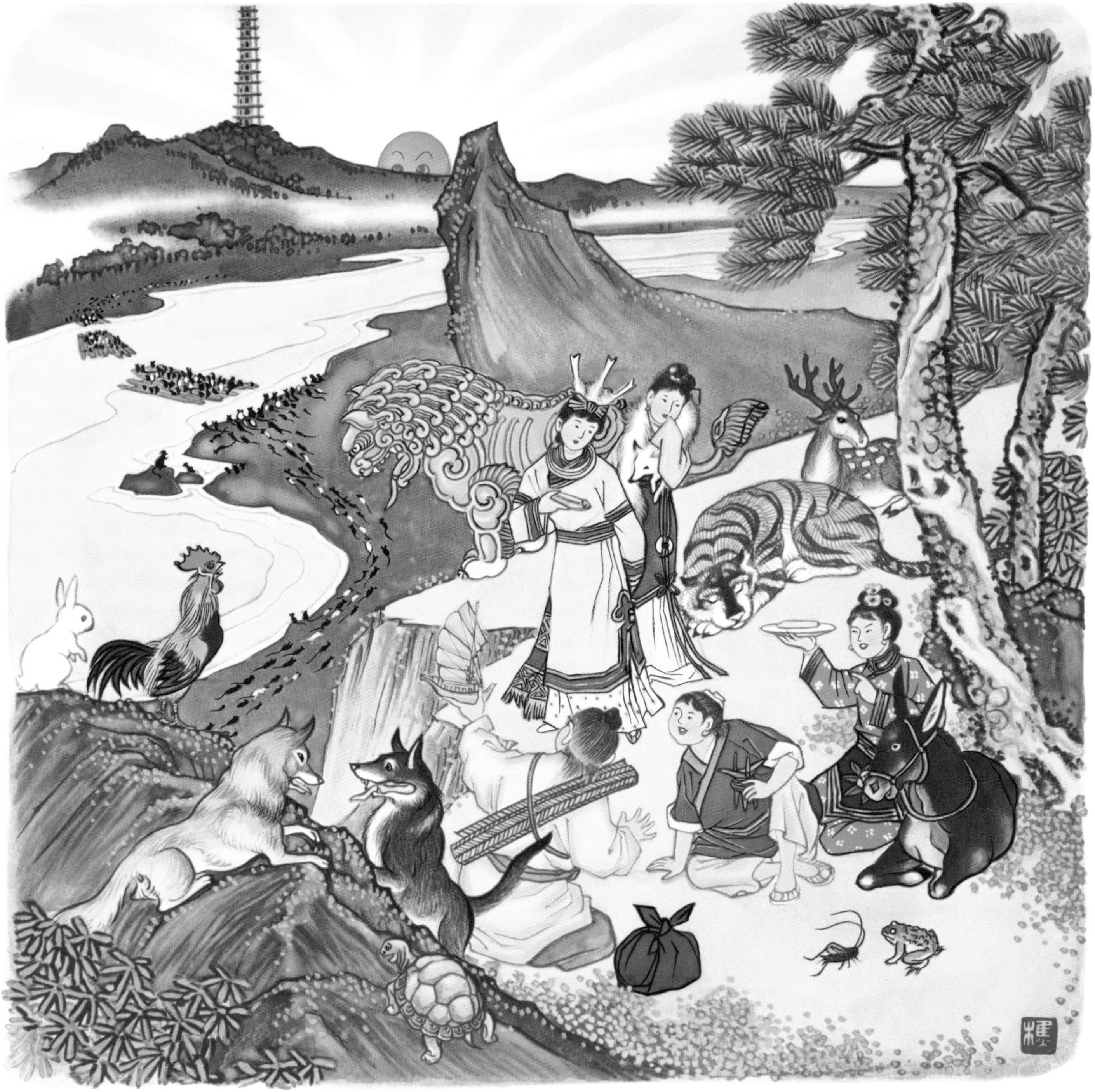

Favorite Children's Stories
from
CHINA and TIBET

by Lotta Carswell Hume

illustrations by Lo Koon-chiu

CHARLES E. TUTTLE COMPANY

Rutland, Vermont & Tokyo, Japan

Published by the Charles E. Tuttle Company, Inc.
of Rutland, Vermont & Tokyo, Japan
with editorial offices at Suido 1-chome, 2-6, Bunkyo-ku, Tokyo

Copyright in Japan, 1962 by Charles E. Tuttle Company, Inc.

All rights reserved

Library of Congress Catalog Card No. 61-6219

International Standard Book No. 0-8048-1605-0

First edition, 1962
First Tuttle paperback edition, 1989
Fourth printing, 1996

PRINTED IN SINGAPORE

Stories in This Book

Publisher's Foreword

Mrs. Lotta Carswell Hume went to Asia first as a bride, accompanying her husband, Dr. Edward H. Hume, who represented the third generation of his family to work as a medical missionary in India. His grandfather, with *his* bride, had sailed to India in 1839 from Salem, Massachusetts, on the brig "Waverly."

After three years in Bombay, Dr. Edward Hume accepted, in 1906, an invitation from Yale University to establish a hospital in Changsha, Hunan Province, in central China. This center became known as Yale-in-China. Here Dr. and Mrs. Hume, with their children, lived for twenty-two years among the Chinese people, coming to know and love them as friends and associates. As Dr. Hume wrote in his own book, *Doctors East, Doctors West:* "Only those can enter effectively into her life who approach China's citadel by way of friendship."

Since their life in China spanned several revolutions, it was a thrilling experience, though sometimes dangerous. Above all, though, it was constantly inspiring to have a part in the development of a China modernizing through introduction into its ancient culture of Western science and medicine.

Mrs. Hume's interest in Chinese stories and legends grew out of her long residence inside the city walls, and her intimate contact with the traditional culture of her Chinese neighbors. Although their home was always in Changsha, the Humes were in contact with Westerners and Chinese from many areas of China. Her stories represent, therefore, traditional tales of various areas, but they are bound together by a quality that is uniquely Chinese. The author has included, as well, some ancient tales from Tibet.

Mrs. Hume speaks in these words of her years in China:

"Our little house in the center of the great walled city of Changsha was surrounded by high walls and every day the voices from the narrow, crowded bustling street came to us over those walls.

"Gradually these voices began to tell us something of our Chinese neighbors and of the fascinating life all about us. As we learned to know our neighbors over the walls better, the city came to be a Story-Book-World, with spirits cavorting up and down the streets—good spirits by day, bad spirits by night—and we were very glad that our house was built with a twisting and turning entrance to keep those bad spirits from rushing inside to catch us.

"It was a Story-Book-World where lightning was the eye of the god looking for evil-doers, and where spirit winds moaned as they flew over the top of our house.

"A Story-Book-World indeed, where we had only to step through the great Moon Gate to reach the Land of Once-Upon-a-Time, where we could hear the stories of Magic Pancakes and Fairy Boats, and could listen to the little animals and big animals telling their wonderful stories; for of course in the Land of Once-Upon-a-Time, all the animals can talk.

"A few of these stories we have caught between the covers of this little book."

Soo Tan the Tiger and the Little Green Frog

∾ Southwest China ∾

ONCE upon a time, when the world was very, very young, men and animals could talk to each other in their forest homes.

Soo Tan was the name of an old tiger who used to wander about in the forest in search of food. One day, as he was snuffling along the banks of a stream, a little frog began to tease him. Perched atop a mound of grass and mud, Master Frog blinked his big, black eyes as he shouted boldly to the tiger: "And where may you be going this bright, beautiful morning?"

To himself, though, Croaky Frog said: "He has certainly come here to eat me, and only my wits can save me."

Soo Tan the tiger answered: "I am going into the forest to get something to eat. For three or four days I haven't eaten a morsel, and I am tired and very hungry. I think I will grab you and eat you, although you are unbearably small, nothing more than an appetizer. But first, tell me who you are."

The little green frog blew up his belly as round as he could and answered in his deepest, croakiest voice: "I am the king of the frogs! I can leap very far indeed, and can do all kinds of wonderful things. Come now, here is a small river—let's have a competition to see which of us can jump farther across it."

Soo Tan answered: "Good, but I must take the first turn."

While the tiger was making ready for his leap, the frog crept around his mound of grass and mud, seized the tip of the tiger's tail, and held fast. Soo Tan took a flying leap to the other bank of the river, unaware that he was carrying the clever little green frog with him.

Proud of his strength and agility, Soo Tan turned to look back toward the water, when, to his surprise, he heard a voice directly behind him.

"What are you looking for, Mr. Tiger?"

There, sitting off in the meadow, far beyond the spot to which the tiger had jumped, sat the little green frog. Soo Tan had no idea of the clever trick by which he had gotten there.

"Well, Mr. Tiger," said the frog, laughing, "since I have beaten you in this competition, let's have another. Let's practice spitting!"

Not to be outwitted by so silly a little creature, the tiger accepted the challenge. But Soo Tan had had nothing to eat. His stomach was quite empty and his

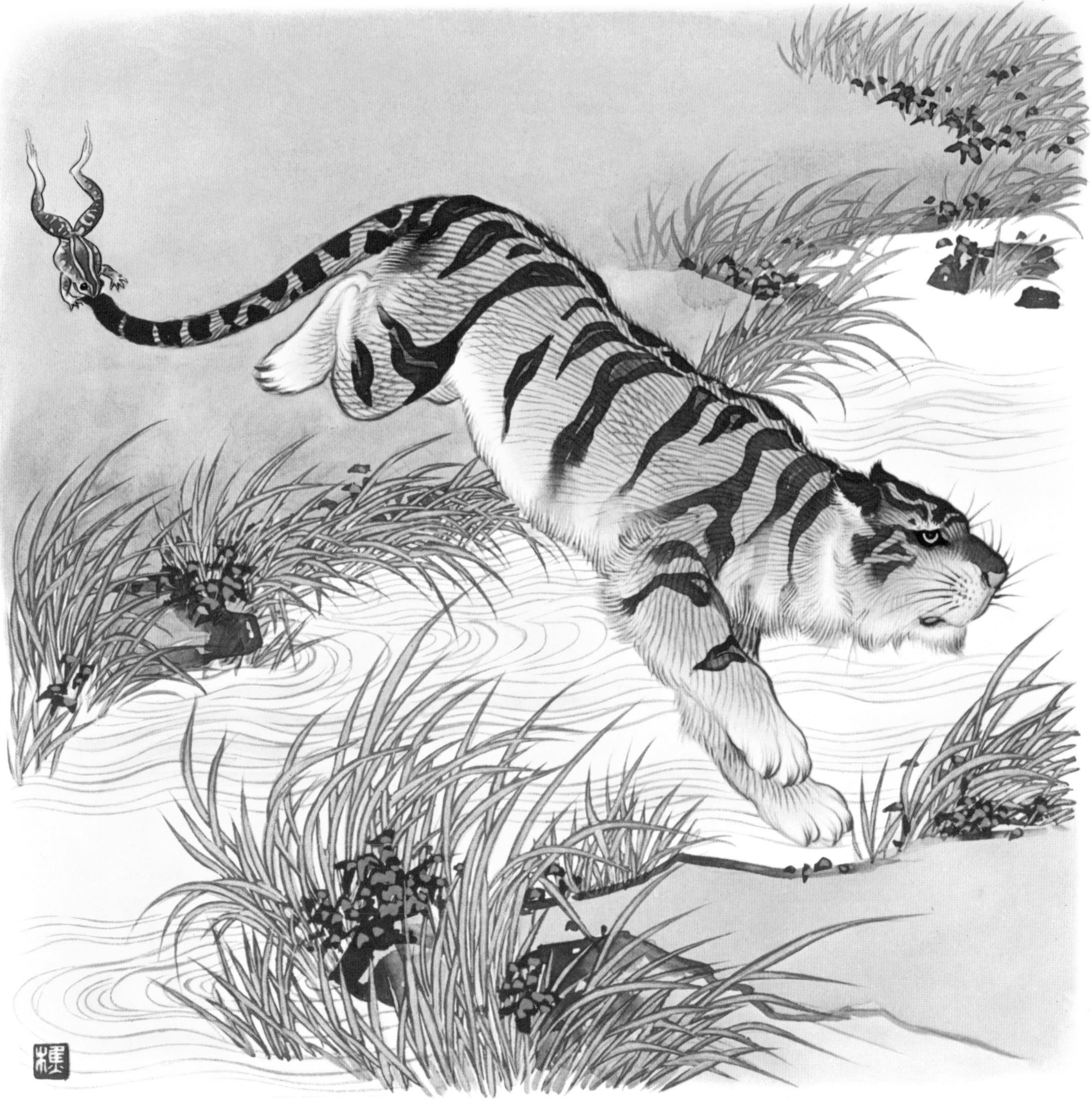

tongue was quite dry, and, try as hard as he would, only a little water trickled from his mouth when he tried to spit.

When the little green frog's turn came, he spat out a great mass of tiger hair, which he had bitten from the end of the tiger's tail as they sailed across the river.

"How does it happen that you have tiger's hair in your stomach?" asked Soo Tan, shaking with fear.

"Oh," said the frog, airily, "yesterday I killed a tiger and ate him, and these are just a few hairs I couldn't digest."

Now Soo Tan thought to himself: "He must be terribly strong indeed to kill a tiger! And today he has jumped farther than I across this stream. I had better escape from him while I can."

So he turned about and fled from the forest. The farther he went, the faster he ran, until finally he reached the very top of the mountain.

As he sat down to catch his breath, he saw his old friend, Mr. Fox, coming down the path.

Soo Tan the Tiger and the Little Green Frog

"What makes you run so fast, Soo Tan?" asked the fox.

"Oh," panted the tiger, "I have seen the king of the frogs. He had just eaten many tigers. He had leaped over the river and was planning to eat me."

The fox laughed at him and said: "You, a great tiger, are running away from a little frog, while I, a small fox, could get him under my foot and stamp him out!"

"If you think you can kill him, I will go back with you," said the tiger. "But, when you see him, I know that you, too, will be afraid and will run away. We had better tie our tails together so that we can help each other."

So the tiger and the fox tied their tails together in strong knots and started off down the mountain to find the little green frog.

The clever little frog sat on his mound of grass and mud, chuckling over the tricks he had played on the great, strong tiger, but, as he sat there ruminating, he watched the path leading out of the deep, dark forest, for he was sure he had not seen the last of Soo Tan.

"Can those two shining green lights possibly be tiger eyes?" he asked himself.

Before he could answer himself, the sharp nose of Mr. Fox appeared, and then the frog saw that, tied to his tail, Mr. Fox dragged along his old enemy, Mr. Tiger.

Then the little green frog shouted in his loudest voice: "You, sir, are a great fox. Today you haven't brought any worthy present to your king. Turn about and look at your tail. Is that a little dog you have brought along for my evening meal?"

Then Soo Tan the tiger was sure that the fox was playing a trick on him and was leading him to the king of the frogs to be killed and devoured. So he turned about and ran with all his might, dragging the fox behind him.

He ran so fast that, if they are not dead now, they are still running through the forest.

But the clever little green frog sat on his mound of grass and mud, blinked his eyes, blew up his belly, and grunted and chuckled at the way he had fooled the great striped tiger.

A Chinese Cinderella

∾ West China ∾

IN THE dim past, before the Ts'in and Han dynasties, there was a chieftain named Wu, who lived in a mountain cave. The people of the countryside called him "Cave Chief Wu."

Now Cave Chief Wu had two wives and a beautiful daughter named Shih Chieh. When this daughter was ten years old, her mother died, and she and her father became close friends. Shih Chieh was not only beautiful; she was clever, as well, and always happy. But one day her father died, and after that

15

the stepmother became so jealous of Shih Chieh's beauty that she sought every possible way to mistreat her. She made the girl cut wood in dangerous places and draw water from deep wells, hoping that some day she would meet with an accident.

One day when Shih Chieh was out in her garden, she caught a beautiful little fish with red fins and golden eyes. It was so tiny that she kept it in a basin in her room. Every day she changed the water in the basin, but at last the fish grew so big that she had no bowl large enough to hold it.

Shih Chieh waited until her cruel stepmother had gone away one day, then she took the fish out and slipped it into the pond in the garden. Every day after that, she crept secretly into the garden to feed the fish scraps of food. So Shih Chieh and the beautiful fish became great friends and when she came to the pond each morning, the fish would swim to the edge of the pool, lift its head from the water, and rest it on the bank as on a pillow.

A Chinese Cinderella

The cruel stepmother somehow heard about the beautiful fish with red fins and golden eyes, and she went often to the garden to try to see it for herself; but the fish would never show itself for anyone but Shih Chieh. The stepmother became very frustrated and angry and secretly determined to kill the fish. One day she said to Shih Chieh: "Aren't you tired today? It is a bright day, so let me wash your coat for you. Go draw water from the neighbor's well. When you return with it, I will wash your coat."

As soon as Shih Chieh had left with her pail, the stepmother hurriedly put on the daughter's clothes and, hiding a sharp sword in her sleeve, she went to the pond and called to the fish. The fish, thinking it was his mistress, raised his head out of the water. Instantly the cruel stepmother drew the sword from her sleeve and killed the fish. She carried it home, cooked it, and ate its delicious meat, then buried the bones under a mound in the field.

The next day Shih Chieh came out to the garden as usual and scattered crumbs on the pool, but the lovely fish with red fins and golden eyes did not come to greet her. Sitting on the bank, she wept piteously. Suddenly a man with tousled hair, and dressed in rough clothing, came down from heaven and comforted her.

"Do not weep, my child. Your mother has killed your fish and hidden its bones under a mound in the field."

Then he leaned close to her and whispered: "I will tell you a great secret. If you will pray to those bones, every wish you have will be granted."

As Shih Chieh turned to thank this stranger, he disappeared from view.

A Chinese Cinderella

Shih Chieh did exactly as the strange visitor had told her. Each day she prayed to the bones of the fish and, just as she had been promised, gold, pearls, and beautiful dresses came to her as soon as she had wished for them.

Now, as it happened, the seventh day of the seventh moon was the day of the Cave Festival. The stepmother took her own daughter, who was not nearly so beautiful as Shih Chieh, and went off to the festival, leaving Shih Chieh behind to tend the house.

"Mind you watch the fruit in the courtyard while we are gone," she called out sharply to Shih Chieh as they went out the gate.

But as soon as they were out of sight, Shih Chieh raced to the mound in the field and asked her fish's bones for a beautiful gown and slippers to wear to the festival. At once she found herself clad in a delectable gown of azure blue and wearing a pair of shining golden slippers. She might have been a fairy queen tripping down the road, so beautiful was she as she followed her mother and sister to the festival.

As she entered the court and joined the dances, everyone turned to look at her, for among all the guests there was no one so lovely as Shih Chieh.

"Why, this girl looks exactly like Shih Chieh," whispered her stepsister. The stepmother scowled in anger. When Shih Chieh saw that they had recognized her, she hurried away from the ball and made haste back to her house. But, in her rush, she dropped one of her golden slippers. The merrymaking was at its height, and no one noticed the Cave Man as he stooped and picked up the shining golden slipper after she had dropped it.

When the stepmother returned home, she found Shih Chieh fast asleep, and she decided that she could not have been at the festival, after all.

The Cave Man's home was on an island on which was the kingdom of T'o Huan, whose military power was the strongest among all the thirty islands in the region. The Cave people sold the golden slipper Shih Chieh had dropped at the festival to the king of T'o Huan.

This king thought that he had never seen anything in his life so lovely as that golden slipper. He was sure that the person who had worn the slipper must be as lovely. The slipper was as light as a moonbeam and it made no sound, even when treading upon stone. So the king sent his heralds to all parts of his realm to ask all the women to try the slipper on. But no one was found who could wear it. Then he commanded the heralds to search every house far and wide to find the mate to the slipper. At last the emissaries returned with the news that another slipper, identical in design, had been found in Shih Chieh's house.

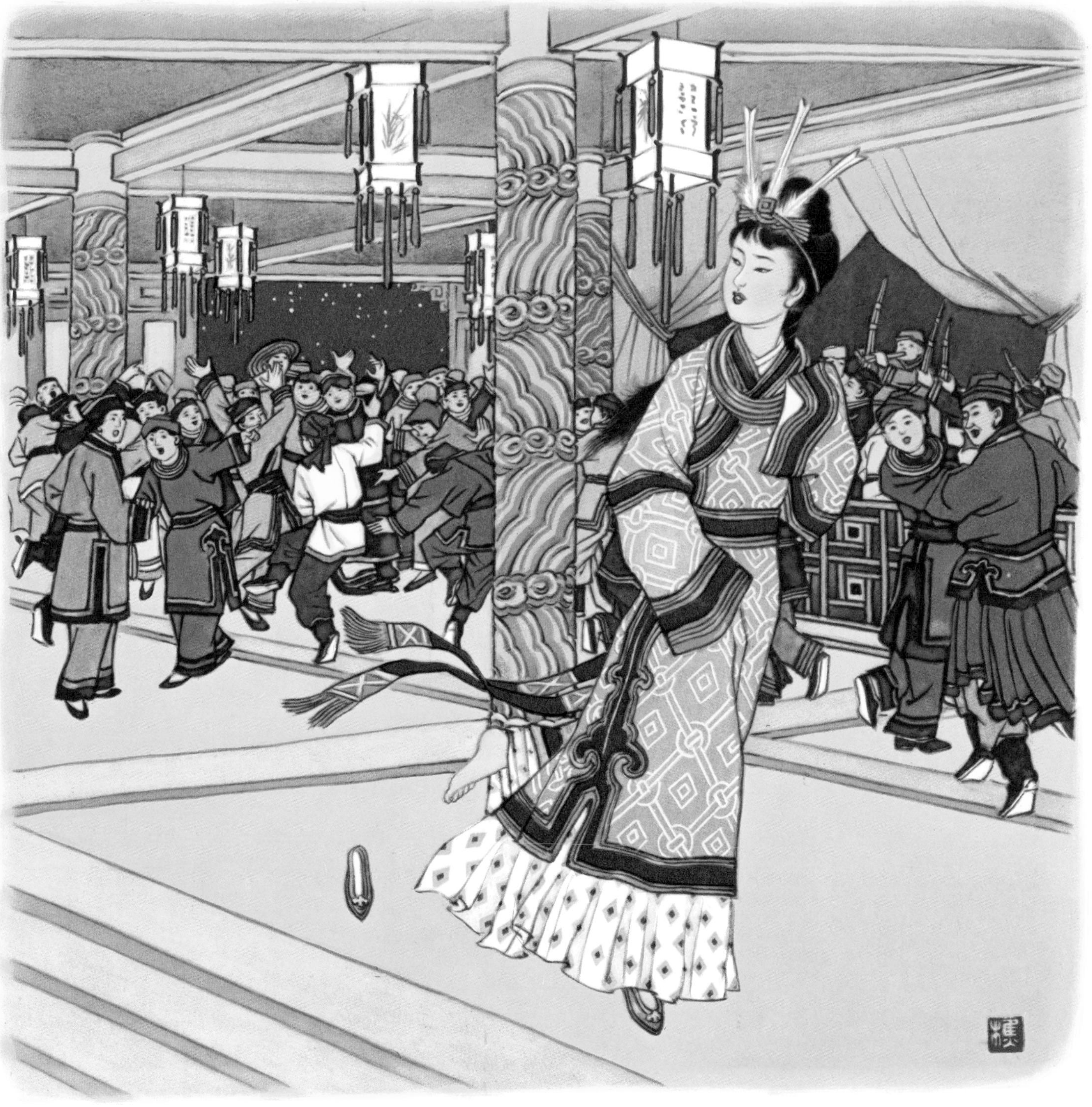

The king of T'o Huan was so excited at this news that he decided to go himself to find the maiden who could wear the slipper.

Shih Chieh hid when she heard that the king was coming, but, when he demanded to see her, she appeared dressed in the same gown of azure blue that she had worn at the festival, and wearing one golden slipper. She looked as beautiful as a goddess, and, when she slipped her slender foot into the lost sandal, it fitted perfectly, and the king bore her away to his kingdom to be his wife. Her stepmother was beside herself with rage and her stepsister wept for a week in annoyance. Before she left, Shih Chieh visited the garden to collect the fish's bones and bring them away with her to her new home.

During the first year of their new life, the king discovered the secret of the fish bones and greedily asked for such an endless number of jewels and jade pieces that the next year his requests went unanswered. Then the king buried the fish bones on the sea coast, together with one hundred bushels of pearls, enclosing them all in a golden parapet.

Several years later the king went back to this spot to unearth the pearls in order to distribute them among his soldiers, who had threatened to rebel. To his dismay, he found that pearls and bones had all been washed away in the tide.

The Fox, the Hare, and the Toad
Have an Argument

∾ Central China ∾

ONE FINE day, a fox, a hare, and a toad were resting themselves under a tree in the forest. In the course of their conversation, they fell to disputing among themselves as to who could trace the longest line of descent.

The fox said: "Bow low, and listen to what I say. My ancestors lived during the great Han Dynasty, as you can see by referring to the classics. Which of

you can boast of so long a line of descent, I should like to know? You must therefore acknowledge that my family is superior to any of yours."

The hare sat on his haunches and stroked his whiskers. Scarcely had the fox finished when he burst into a loud laugh and said: "You are quite an upstart and, like all of that class, you make yourself ridiculous. Long before the Han Dynasty was ever dreamed of, there was a moon, you must acknowledge. If you look at the moon on any clear night, you will see a cinnamon tree, beneath which is a hare pounding medicines in a mortar. This is my distinguished forebear. It seems to me you must admit that my family line is the longest and the most respectable."

The fox was silent, but the toad laughed until the tears ran down his cheeks;

and it was some time before he could sober himself sufficiently to tell *his* story: "Long before ever the moon existed, and when the heavens were first formed out of chaos, there lived three brother toads. One of them met his death by being crushed beneath one of the pillars of heaven; another died when Pandora melted the five stones with which she repaired a rent in the heavens; and the third was killed when the first Emperor of Chiu built his great palace. How can I avoid laughing when I hear such upstarts as you two make claims to long line and respectability!"

Now, while the toad was boasting of his noble ancestors, a tiger had slyly joined the group, and when the toad had finished speaking, the tiger quietly stretched out his paw and brushed the toad to one side with a sniff of contempt.

"Oh, Mr. Tiger," said the toad, "we are not discussing feats of strength, my most noble sir. We are talking about respectability."

"Well, now," replied the tiger, "since you have such a contempt for strength, perhaps you can tell me what would happen to you if I were to place a single one of my paws on you and keep it there for a few days?"

The Fox, the Hare, and the Toad Have an Argument   25

The toad thought deeply for a moment and then he answered: "I could easily live by swallowing my own saliva, for toads rarely partake of anything else. But, my noble sir, may I ask what would become of *you* while you were holding me under your paw? For tigers, unlike toads, must have more material nourishment than saliva, and I greatly fear that you would starve to death." The tiger could not reply to this argument and he turned about and walked away.

The fox, the hare, and the toad waited until the tiger was well out of sight; then they laughed till their sides shook at the clever answer of the toad. When they calmed down, they all agreed that the best thing for them to do was to disappear into the forest themselves, before the tiger had time to think the whole thing over and decide to come back to enjoy a good supper.

The Fox, the Hare, and the Toad Have an Argument

How the Cock Got His Red Crown

∾ West China ∾

FAR IN the west of China, the Miao tribespeople watch the sun sink behind the rugged mountains of Tibet, and, as the shadows lengthen across the sun-baked court, they gather to hear the village storyteller relate again the legends of their tribe.

Long, long ago, when the world had just been made, this great land had six suns, instead of one sun, shining in the sky. One spring, after the farmers had put in hard weeks of sowing crops, the rains refused to come at their appointed time, and the blazing of the six big suns dried up every tender shoot.

Now, the great Yao was emperor of China at this time, and when he saw this he was filled with sorrow. He said to his courtiers: "If the six suns continue shining like this, my people will all die." But still, day after day, the six suns rose high in the heavens and burned up the crops.

Then the ten wise old elders of the village gathered to discuss what could be done to save their crops.

At length one old man said: "The only way is to shoot the suns."

When Emperor Yao heard this, he was greatly moved. He sent his courtiers far and wide to select the best archers in the kingdom and to summon them to the court.

The archers were strong. Each one carried his great bow slung over his shoulder as he came proudly to serve the great emperor.

How the Cock Got His Red Crown

The people of the village and the ten wise old men gathered under the burning skies to watch the archers test their skill. As soon as Emperor Yao appeared, they let loose their arrows. But alas, although their bows were strong and their arrows swift, they did not reach even halfway to the six suns blazing in the heavens.

In great humility then, the archers bowed low before the emperor and said: "However accurately we shoot at them, the suns will remain, for no arrow can reach them."

Then, from afar, came other men to the court and said: "Prince Howee of the neighboring kingdom is skilled as an archer. Invite him to come."

So Emperor Yao again sent forth his heralds and summoned Prince Howee of the neighboring tribe to the palace.

Once again the people thronged under the burning skies, this time to see if the arrows of Howee could reach the suns. When everyone was assembled, Emperor Yao commanded: "Shoot down the six suns and save my people!"

Howee looked at the suns and he lifted his bow; but then he turned sadly to the emperor and said: "The six suns are too far away for my slender arrows to reach."

Just then, however, Howee saw the six bright suns reflected in a pool, and he thought: "It will be just the same to shoot them there."

So he drew his bow, and his arrow pierced the first sun, which disappeared into the bottom of the pool. He fired again, and the second sun disappeared, then the third, and the fourth, and the fifth sun.

When the sixth sun saw what was happening, he became so scared that he disappeared over the hill. The ten village elders were quite content that the six suns had all been driven away, so the people returned each to his own mud hut.

But when the villagers awakened from their long sleep, there was no "next day," for the sixth sun was afraid to come forth from the cave in which he was hiding and shine again on the earth. So the ten old men gathered again in the darkness to see what could be done. They all decided that they had best find someone to summon the sixth sun out from his hiding place so that there could be a "next day."

First they brought a tiger, and he roared and roared to the sixth sun to come out, but the sixth sun only became very angry at his roaring, and he said: "I won't come out!"

Then they brought a cow, thinking that the gentle lowing of a cow would

How the Cock Got His Red Crown

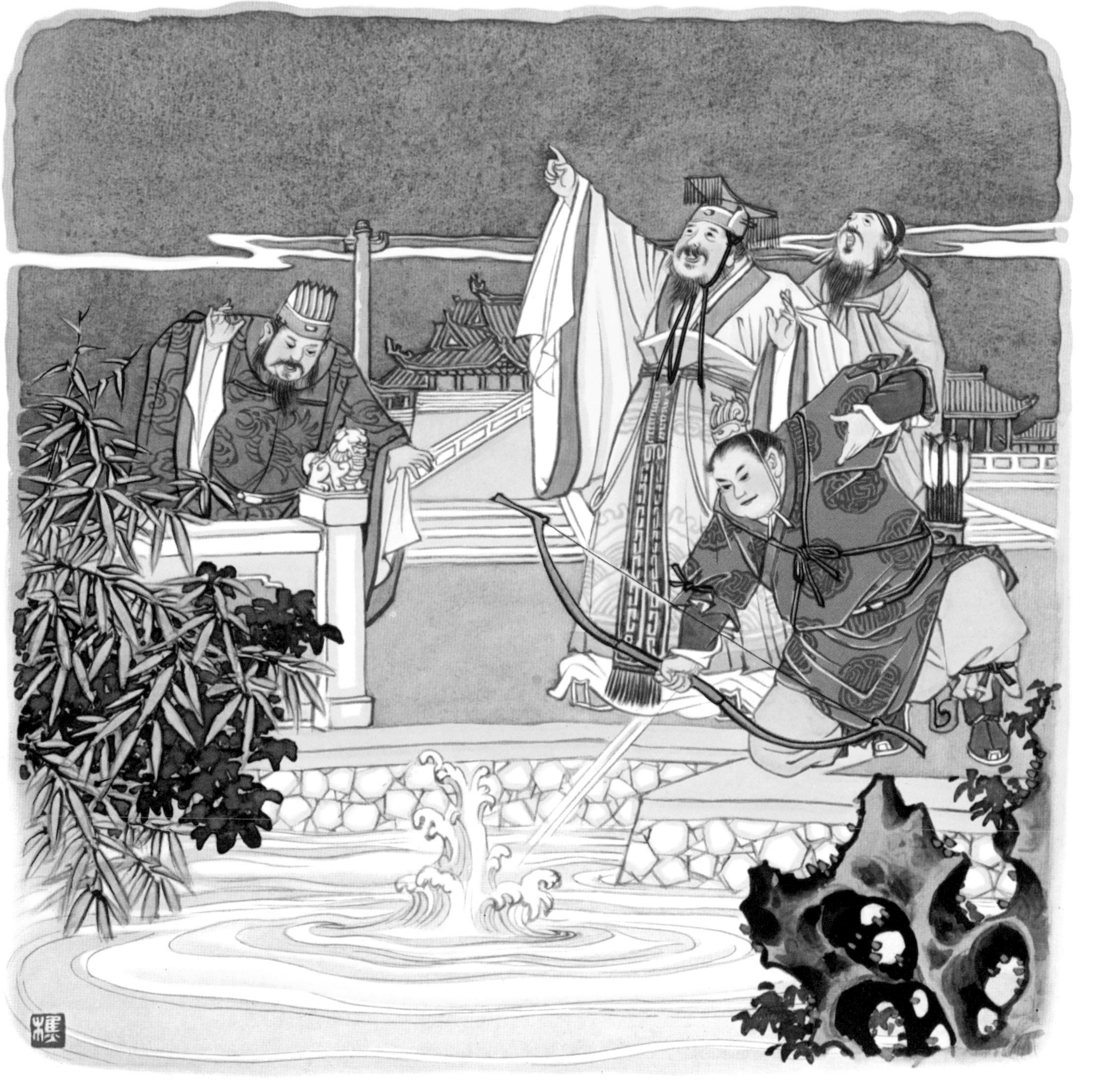

surely lure the sun forth, but the sixth sun was still angry and sulking, and he said again: "I won't come out, so there!"

At last they brought a fine fat cock to crow, and the sixth sun listened, and then he said: "What lovely sound!" And he peeked out over the horizon to see what could be making it.

As he peered down at them, the people all saw him, and they shouted glad shouts of welcome and joy. The sixth sun was so pleased that he came out all the way, and then he fashioned a little red crown for the head of the fine fat cock.

And every morning since that faraway day, the cock wears his red crown when he crows to call forth the sun.

How the Cock Got His Red Crown

The Cricket Fight

∾ *North China* ∾

ONCE upon a time there lived a little cricket called Guitar Wing. He lived with his brothers behind the rocks in Farmer Wang's field. His name was not yet Guitar Wing when he lived there. He got that name after he had become a famous fighting cricket; on the great day, in fact, when he downed Yellow Bald Head.

From the time when this cricket was a baby, he had heard Grandfather tell the story of *his* big fight—how scared Grandfather Cricket was when the fight began, but how proud he grew when the crowd shouted his name and called him a great hero.

So Guitar Wing said to himself: "Some day I am certainly going to be a great fighter like Old Grandfather." Since he knew that the cricket that chirped loudest would be selected when the men came to hunt champion crickets, he tried every day to chirp louder and louder and shriller and shriller. He also took big jumps daily to make his legs strong. He worked so hard that he thought some day his chirps might even drown out the croaking of old Grumpy Frog in the next pond. Every time he thought of the way that Grumpy Frog had got his croak, he had to laugh.

Grandfather Cricket had told him that story. He had said that once upon a faraway time, a man and his little wife were walking together across a bridge. The little wife was carrying in her arms a huge melon, called a *gwa;* her husband had a long staff, called a *gwer.* When they got to the middle of the bridge, they stopped to look over the railing. The little wife accidentally dropped her

melon into the water. The old man tried to get it back with his staff, but it slipped out of his hand, so his staff was lost, as well. Since the old man could not walk without his staff, he leaned 'way over to try to catch it, and he, too, fell into the water. When the little wife tried to rescue him, in *she* went, and they were both drowned.

The gods, who are interested in the doings of world-people, had watched this couple's devotion for many years, so, in pity, they changed them into frogs in order that they might continue to live together. From that day on, the old woman frog cries: "Gwa-Gwa! I want my Gwa!" And the old man frog shouts hoarsely: "GWER! GWER!" So, when anyone is near the river, he can hear them croaking, Gwa-Gwer-Gwa-GWER-GWA-GWER!

Guitar Wing laughed, too, at his silly cousins, the Singing Crickets, for he had heard that they were kept as pets by old Chinese scholars, who carried them about in the folds of their wadded gowns, or kept them sitting on their writing desks. Such a dull life to live!

But this was no time for laughing idly at Croaky Frog, or at his silly singing cousins, for already it was the Ninth Moon—sometimes called the Chrysanthemum Moon—when the great cricket fights would begin.

One day, just after Guitar Wing had breakfasted deliciously upon a big fat grub, he heard the pounding of a great man-giant's feet on the rocks. "Now is my chance," he thought. "They have come to look for fighters!" So he chirped just about the loudest chirp that had ever been heard, and presto, ker-plunk, before he had time to even wonder what was happening, a big net was popped over his head, and he was thrown into a basket. This did seem a strange way to be treated, and Guitar Wing was beginning to be a bit angry, but, just then, he heard the man-giant, who was carrying the basket on a bamboo pole, say that there would certainly be hundreds of other men-giants watching the fight, and that they would be certain to pay much money to the owner of the cricket who won. When he heard this, Guitar Wing forgot to be angry or upset. He busied himself climbing up and down the basket to make his legs very strong.

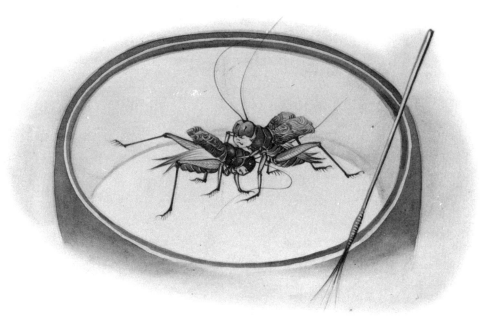

This is how Guitar Wing tells his own story of what happened to him at the end of that ride in the basket.

"First, the men put me into a little earthenware pot, lined with soft mould; then they gave me the best things to eat, fish, and nice fat grubs, boiled chestnuts, and rice with honey, to make me strong. Once, when I ate too much and got very sick, they made me eat a red insect called a *hun-ch'ung,* but this didn't taste very good. I heard them say that if I caught cold, I was to get mosquitoes, but I never did catch cold.

"When the day of the fight came, it seemed to me that everyone in the world was crowded around the bowl that they called the 'Cricket Pit.' What a fight we had that day, Yellow Bald Head and I! First we glared at each other, until a man-giant tickled our backs with some scratchy pig bristles. Then we got very excited, and rushed at each other, and down I went. I heard the men shouting: 'Up, Guitar Wing!' I was too angry and excited to stay down. It was a hard fight, all right, but before long, I had *him* down, and finally I left Yellow Bald Head lying in the bottom of the old brown bowl, minus a leg or two.

"As they carried me away, the crowd shouted, and I felt very happy to be a great hero, just like Grandfather.

"I never again saw my brothers, for I was kept to win other fights. It was fine to be a hero, but sometimes, when I heard the chirping away off in Farmer Wang's field, I wondered whether, after all, it might not be better to be just a Singing Cricket, sitting on the desk of the old Chinese scholar, or wrapped snugly in the folds of his warm padded gown."

The Story of the Tortoise and the Monkey

∾ Tibet ∾

THERE was once an old tortoise who lived with his wife and family in a large lake, on the borders of which grew an extensive jungle; and in the forest there were many wild beasts, more especially, monkeys, who swarmed in great numbers all along the shores of the lake.

It happened one day that the tortoise came out of the lake and went for a stroll among the trees which grew near the water. After walking for some distance, he became hungry, and looking up into a coconut tree, near which he found himself, he thought how much he should like to get one of the coconuts which were growing near the top. He made several awkward attempts to climb the tree, but the stem was so straight and so smooth that he was quite unable to succeed; and he was just about to give up the attempt in despair when he spied a large monkey sitting among the branches. The monkey, who had been watching with some curiosity the tortoise's attempts to climb the tree, felt rather sorry at his failure, and noticing that the tortoise was a fine, well-grown fellow with a very handsome shell, he thought he would do him a kindness. So, breaking off one or two of the coconuts, he threw them down to the tortoise, who gratefully ate the fruit.

The two animals now entered into conversation with one another, and soon striking up quite a friendship, the monkey led the tortoise away into the jungle and showed him a comfortable cave where he could spend the night. The tortoise was so interested in all he saw, and so pleased with his friend the monkey, that he remained for several days in the forest, moving about during the day and sleeping with the monkey in the cave every night.

Meanwhile Mrs. Tortoise was becoming rather anxious concerning her husband's prolonged absence. He had never been away from home for so long before, so finally she dispatched one of the young tortoises to find out where his father was and how he was getting on. The young tortoise accordingly swam to land, and after hunting about for some time in the forest, he came across his father near the cave.

"Good morning, Father," said he, "Mother has sent me to find out where you are and how you are getting on."

"Oh, I am all right, my boy," replied Father Tortoise, "tell Mother she need

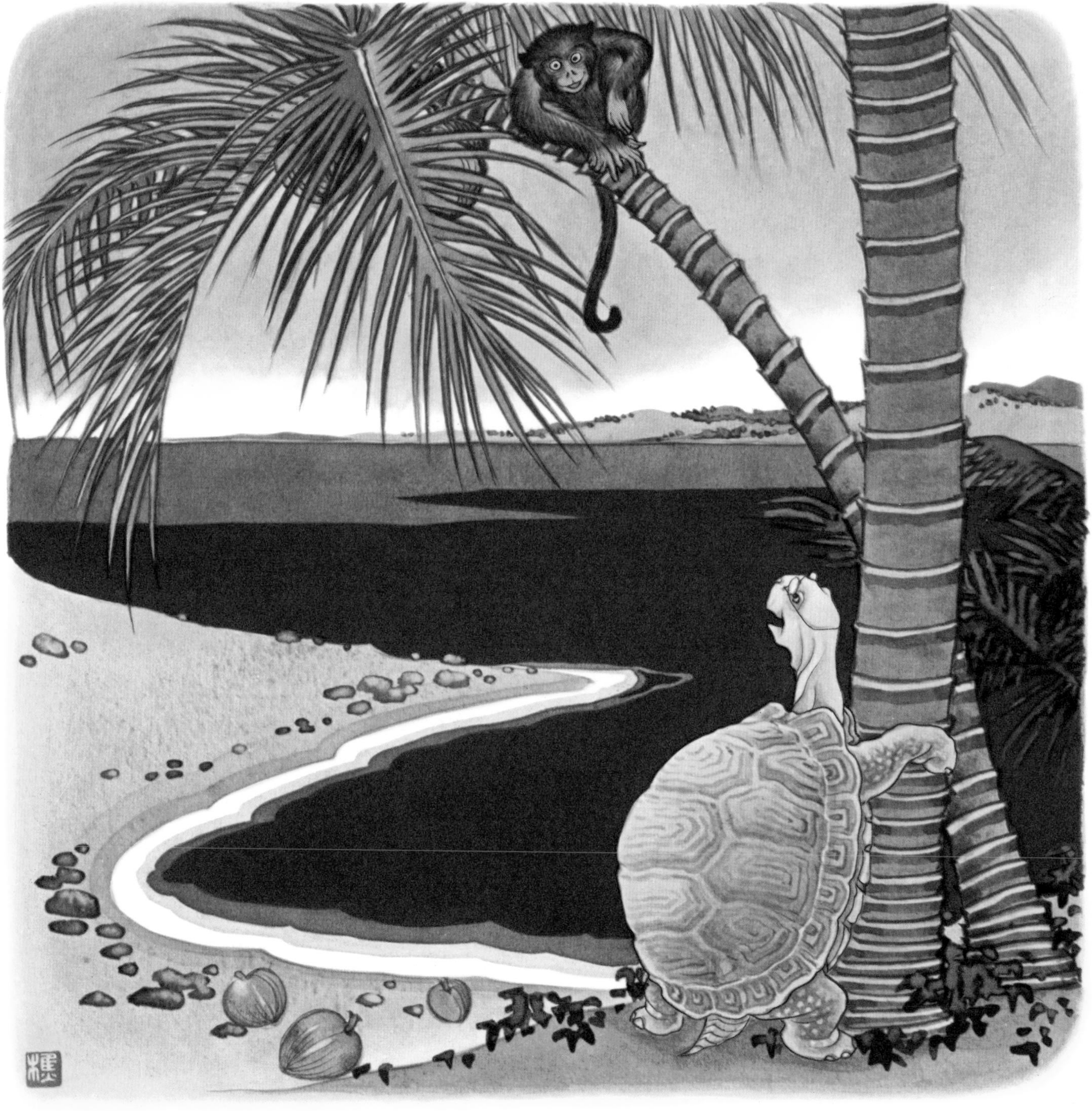

not trouble about me. My friend, Brother Monkey, and I are just having a good time in the forest, and I will be home in a few days. Now run off to your mother."

So the young tortoise went back to his mother and told her what had happened. Mrs. Tortoise was not at all pleased at her husband's conduct.

"It is quite time," thought she, "that he should return to his wife and family, instead of amusing himself with a vulgar monkey in the forest."

So she sent the boy back again to his father, with a message to say that Mrs. Tortoise was very ill, and that her physician had told her that the only thing to cure her was a monkey's heart. Therefore he must return at once to his home and bring a monkey along with him.

The young tortoise accordingly proceeded to hunt out his father again, and as soon as he met him, he gave him Mrs. Tortoise's message. On hearing the news of his wife's illness, Mr. Tortoise became much alarmed, and reproached himself for having stayed away for so long; and in order to secure the necessary medicine for his wife, he informed his friend the monkey that he was obliged to return home at once on urgent business, and he invited the monkey to come and spend a few days at his house. The monkey accepted his friend's invitation, and the two set off together to the shores of the lake.

When the monkey understood that it would be necessary for him to enter the lake, he became rather alarmed, and remarked to the tortoise that never having been in the water, he was afraid it would be difficult for him to reach the tortoise's home.

"Never fear about that, Brother Monkey," said the tortoise, "I can arrange that quite simply. If you will mount upon my back, I will swim with you wherever we want to go."

So the monkey mounted upon the tortoise's back, and the tortoise set out to swim to his house.

As they went across the lake, the tortoise began telling the monkey about his wife's illness, and in doing so, he foolishly let slip that the only medicine to

cure her was a monkey's heart. On hearing this, the monkey became very much alarmed, and saw that he was being led into a trap.

"Dear me, Brother Tortoise," said he, "I am very much grieved to hear of your wife's illness, but if she is as bad as all that, I do not think that one monkey's heart will be enough. I should think that three or four, at least, would be required in order to effect a cure. If you like, I can easily get several other monkeys from among my friends to accompany us to your home."

The tortoise thought that this was a good idea, and agreed to carry the monkey back to the shore and to await him there while he went off to fetch some other monkeys. So he turned round and swam back through the lake till he reached the edge, where he waddled out on to the beach.

As soon as he found himself on dry land, the monkey skipped off the tortoise's back as fast as he could, and climbed in a twinkling to the top of the tallest tree he could find. On reaching the top of the tree, he began reviling the tortoise, and calling out every bad name he could think of.

"You are a nice sort of friend," said he, "to ask me to pay a visit to your home in order to kill me and use my heart as medicine for your ugly wife. Do you call that a proper return for all my attention to you, and for showing you all over the jungle? However, I have been too clever for you this time, and you will have to do without my heart for many a long day to come.

And as to the hearts of those other monkeys that I promised to you—well, you can just wait till you find them for yourself!"

The tortoise, on hearing these words, fell into a violent passion, and made several efforts to climb the tree in order to punish the monkey, but being quite unable to climb at all, he soon gave up his attempt and determined to get even with the monkey in some other way.

So he hid himself in the water until evening, and as soon as it was dusk, he came out on the land and proceeded very quietly to the cave where he and the monkey had lived together, and concealed himself in the darkest corner of it, waiting till the monkey should come in.

The monkey, however, was a good deal too clever to be caught in a simple trap like this. When his usual bedtime arrived, he came to the mouth of the cave and looking in, he called out in a loud voice: "Oh, great cave! great cave!"

The tortoise lay low in his dark corner and gave no sign of life.

After a few moments' silence, the monkey again called out: "Oh, great cave! great cave!"

Still the tortoise lay low and gave no sign.

"Curious thing," said the monkey to himself in an audible tone of voice, "very curious! There used always to be an echo in this cave, but I can't hear the slightest echo tonight. There must be something wrong." After saying this, he called out again: "Oh great cave! great cave!"

The foolish tortoise, thinking that if he simulated an echo the monkey would enter the cave as usual, hereupon gave answer from his dark corner: "Oh great cave! great cave!"

On hearing this, the monkey chuckled to himself at the simplicity of the tortoise, and went off to sleep in some other part of the forest.

The Wishing Cup

∾ South China ∾

ONCE on a time there was a little boy named Hsiao Lung, which means "Little Dragon." He lived with his mother, his big sister "Lilac Blossom," his little sister Chen Chu (which means "A Pearl"), and his old grannie, his spotted pig, and his chickens.

They were very poor indeed, and their little brown hut had only one door, and two tiny windows with paper instead of glass in them to keep out the cold winds.

47

Spotted Pig grunted an angry grunt every evening when he saw the chickens hop in through the door to sleep warm under Grannie's bed, while he had to stay outside in the cold. But he was glad in the morning when he was the only one at the gate to watch Little Dragon start out with his lantern, long before the rooster had come out to crow his announcement to the people that it was the next day and time to get up.

Hsiao Lung worked all day long in the rice fields, transplanting the tender little rice shoots. He knew that if he started very early, and worked hard and long, the farmer would give him a big sack of rice for his mother to cook for Grannie and Lilac Blossom and Chen Chu.

When Hsiao Lung set forth, it was so dark as he followed the winding path between the rice fields that the pools of water on each side of the path looked like great wells of ink. He swung his lantern very low, to throw its light on the narrow path, for it was wet and slippery and he did not want to fall into

the pools of inky water. Spotted Pig watched him as the lantern swung along the path and then climbed up and up the steep hill. When the little light disappeared over the top of the hill, he grunted and turned away.

One day, after Hsiao Lung had been working at a farm a long way from his home, he found it was too late to go back to his little mud house to sleep, for already darkness was shutting in all the hill. He wondered what to do.

"I will lose my way if I try to go home," he sobbed. "But here I have no place to sleep. What shall I do? What SHALL I do?"

Just then the bell in the temple rang to call the priests to prayer. Hsiao Lung had heard this bell before, many times; but this time it seemed to be speaking directly to him, and to say: "Come and sleep in the temple with me. Come and sleep in the temple with me."

So Hsiao Lung followed the sound of the bell until he reached the great red painted gate of the temple. The temple courts were very still as Hsiao Lung peered through the gate, for the priests were chanting their prayers in an inner room.

He pushed through the gate and looked about to see where he might hide. Just then the chanting stopped, and he heard a door creak. So Hsiao Lung jumped into a closet and shut the door very softly.

The little closet was so dark and the temple so quiet that Hsiao Lung began to think of his mother, and of Lilac Blossom and Chen Chu and Grannie and the spotted pig and the chickens; he thought so hard that a big tear ran down the end of his nose and splashed off in the dark!

Suddenly he heard voices. The priests, who were really the Eight Fairies, had started to play a game of chess. Hsiao Lung was happy to hear them laughing over their game, but all of a sudden he heard one of them say: "I smell a mortal!" Then another one said: "I smell a mortal!" Then Hsiao Lung became so frightened that he shook all over, from his head right down to his feet. He shook and he shook, but, since no one opened his little closet door, he put his ear to the crack of the door to catch what the priests were saying. This is what he heard: "Do not forget, O fellow Fairies, that the Wishing Cup is hidden under the big rock at the southeast corner of the temple wall. And remember, too, that if anyone taps the cup, it will grant any wish that is made—yes, any wish at all."

Little Dragon was so excited by this fine secret he had heard that he could scarcely wait for the Eight Fairies to go to bed so that he could investigate and find out if what they said was really true. When he heard the fairies snor-

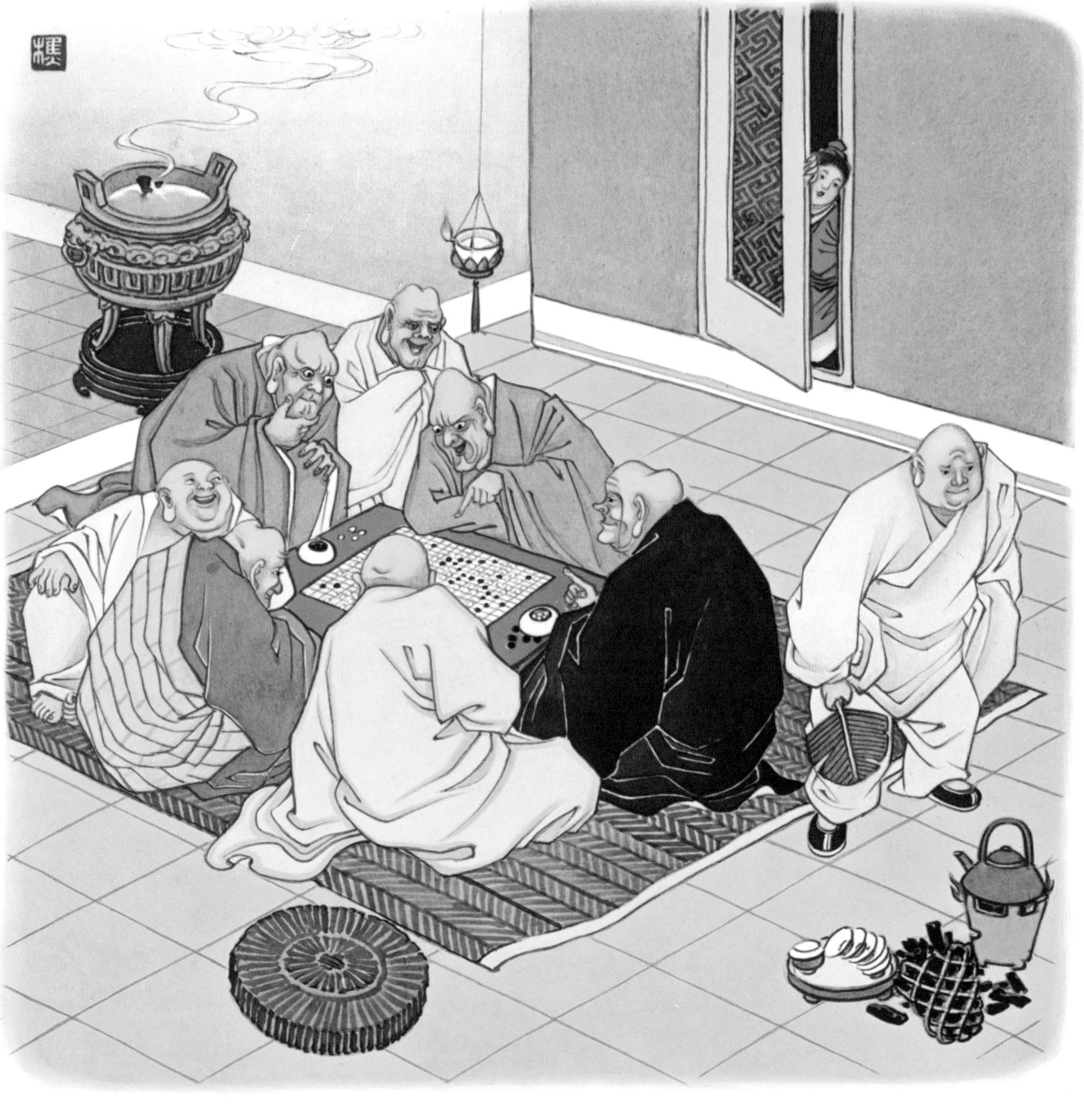

ing, he crept very softly from the closet and tiptoed to the southeast corner of the temple wall. There he saw a big stone, and, lifting it, he discovered under it the very cup they had described. Now all his fear was forgotten. Singing and prancing like a wild colt, he ran all the way home, hugging his treasure. He arrived there just as the family were dividing the last bit of rice.

Hsiao Lung knew exactly what to wish for. Tap, tap, he rapped his knuckle against the cup. "I wish for a feast of every good thing to come to this table." At once there sprang up meats and drinks and cakes and sweets, and the family feasted as they had never done before in their lives. When they couldn't eat another morsel, they summoned the neighbors and urged them to eat all *they* wanted. And they gave each a bundle of goodies to carry home. Then they sat and listened again to the strange story that Hsiao Lung had heard through the

crack of the closet door. Grannie beamed contentedly, his mother wept for joy, Lilac Blossom and Chen Chu danced about, the chickens cackled with glee, and Spotted Pig grunted in delight.

The very next day one of the neighbors, a loutish fellow named Wu, decided that he should have the same good fortune; so he stole away early to the temple and hid himself in the same closet. By and by, he heard the Eight Fairies at their game of chess, and then one of them said: "I smell a mortal!" Before Wu knew what was happening, the closet door flew open and the Eight Fairies dragged him out. "Ah ha, a mortal is hiding in our closet!" cried one of the fairies, and he pulled Wu's nose, and pulled and pulled some more until he had pulled it out a foot long. Then another of the fairies pulled it out another foot, and then another and another, until the Eight Fairies had pulled Wu's nose out eight feet. Poor Wu went back to his village disgraced, dragging his nose behind him; and all the children gathered and pointed and laughed at his funny nose, eight feet long and dragging in the dust!

But Little Dragon's mother insisted that he return the cup next day to its hiding place because of the ill luck it had brought to Neighbor Wu.

Little Dragon, too, felt sorry for his friend, Wu, so that night, after everyone had gone to bed, he took out the wishing cup and rapped on it again with his knuckles. Tap, tap, tap. "I wish that Wu's nose would grow short again."

Next morning when Wu woke up, he felt for his long nose and found that it had disappeared during the night.

A Hungry Wolf

∾ Tibet ∾

ONE DAY, in the upper part of a Tibetan valley, high above the cultivated fields, a hungry wolf was prowling about searching something to eat. All at once he came upon a rather delicious looking donkey, about a year old. At once the wolf proceeded to stalk the donkey, thinking that he would make an excellent meal from him.

Just as he was about to seize him, the donkey noticed his approach and addressed him as follows: "Oh, Uncle Wolf, it is surely no good your eating me now. This is the springtime, and after the long, hard winter I am still very thin. If you will but wait for a few months, until next autumn, you will find me twice as fat as I am now, and I shall make you a much better feast."

"Very well," replied the wolf. "I will wait until then, on condition that you meet me on this spot in six months' time."

And so saying, he galloped off in search of some other prey.

In no time at all, the leaves had turned and autumn had come round. One fine morning, exactly six months later, the wolf started off to meet the donkey at the appointed spot. As he was loping along, drooling with anticipation, he came upon a fox.

"Good morning, Brother Wolf," said the fox. "Where are you off to this fine brisk morning?"

"Oh," replied the wolf, "I am going into the valley where I have an appointment with a donkey. I have an arrangement to eat him this very day."

"How pleasant for you, Brother Wolf," answered the fox. "But as the don-

A Hungry Wolf

key is such a large animal, you will scarcely be able to eat him all by yourself without getting a bad case of indigestion. I think you should let me accompany you and share in your feast."

The wolf was in a hospitable mood. "Certainly, Brother Fox," he replied. "I'll be glad to have your company."

So the two went on together. After they had proceeded a short distance, they came upon a hare.

"Good morning, Brother Wolf and Brother Fox," said the hare in greeting. "Where are you going this lovely day?"

"Good morning, Brother Hare," replied the wolf. "I am just going off into yonder valley to keep an appointment with a fat donkey whom I have arranged to eat for my dinner today. Brother Fox is coming along with me as my guest."

"Oh, really, Brother Wolf?" responded the hare "Well, I do wish you would ask me along, too. A donkey is really too large for even the two of you, and you could well afford to let such a small creature as I share in a bit of the spoil."

"Why certainly, Brother Hare," replied the wolf, who was in a mellow mood. "We shall be delighted to have you accompany us."

And so the three animals went on together to the appointed spot. When they approached the place, they saw the young donkey waiting for them. During the summer months he had consumed a quantity of grass and had become fat and sleek, and almost twice as big as he had been in the spring. When the wolf caught sight of him he could scarcely contain his delight and he began to lick his chops in anticipation.

"Well, Brother Donkey," he said affably. "Here I am, according to our agreement, ready to eat you. I am happy to see you looking so plump and well. Here are Brother Fox and Brother Hare who have come along with me for a bite to eat."

And so saying, the wolf crouched down, ready to spring upon the donkey.

"Wait a moment, Brother Wolf," called out the hare at this moment. "I have a suggestion to make. It seems to me it would be a pity for you to kill this fine young donkey in the usual way, by seizing his throat, for if you do, a great deal of his blood will be wasted. I should like to suggest, as a better plan, that you strangle him, for in that situation no blood will be lost, and we shall then derive the full benefit from his carcass."

The wolf straightened up and thought this over. Then he said: "Well, Brother Hare, that's an excellent idea. I wonder why I didn't think of it myself. But how is it to be done?"

"Easily enough," answered the hare. "Over yonder is a shepherd's encampment. There we can borrow a rope, in which we will make a slipknot, put the loop over the donkey's head, and pull as hard as we can."

So they all agreed on this plan. Brother Fox was dispatched to the encampment to borrow a rope from the shepherd and he carried it back to where his companions were waiting.

"Now," said the hare, "here is our procedure. We will put this large slipknot over the donkey's neck, and as he is so large and heavy, we must all three pull together at the other end of the rope. So you, Brother Wolf, and you, Brother

Fox, put your heads through these smaller loops I have fixed; I will seize the loose end of the rope with my teeth, and when I give the signal, let us all pull together."

The other two fell in with this plan at once. So they threw the slipknot over the donkey's neck and the wolf and the fox put their heads through the smaller loops. When they were all ready, the hare took up his position at the end of the rope, and caught hold of it with his protruding front teeth.

"Now," said he, "are you ready?"

"Yes, ready," answered the wolf.

"Yes, quite ready," echoed the fox.

"Well, then, pull," said the hare.

So they began to pull, just as hard as they could. When the donkey felt the pull on the rope, he walked forward a few paces, much to the surprise of the wolf and the fox, who felt themselves being dragged along the ground.

"Pull, can't you!" shrieked the wolf, as the rope began to tighten around his neck.

"Pull yourself!" shrieked back the fox, who was now beginning to feel very uncomfortable, with the blood pounding in his forehead.

"Pull, all of you," called out the hare, and with that, he let go the end of the rope and the donkey galloped off, dragging the fox and the wolf after him. In a few moments, both were strangled soundly. The donkey, shaking off the rope from his neck, pulled back his lips and gave one loud "hee-haw" up the valley. Then he proceeded to graze quietly in his usual pastures.

The hare twitched his nose in amusement, then scampered off home, feeling that he had done an admirable day's work.

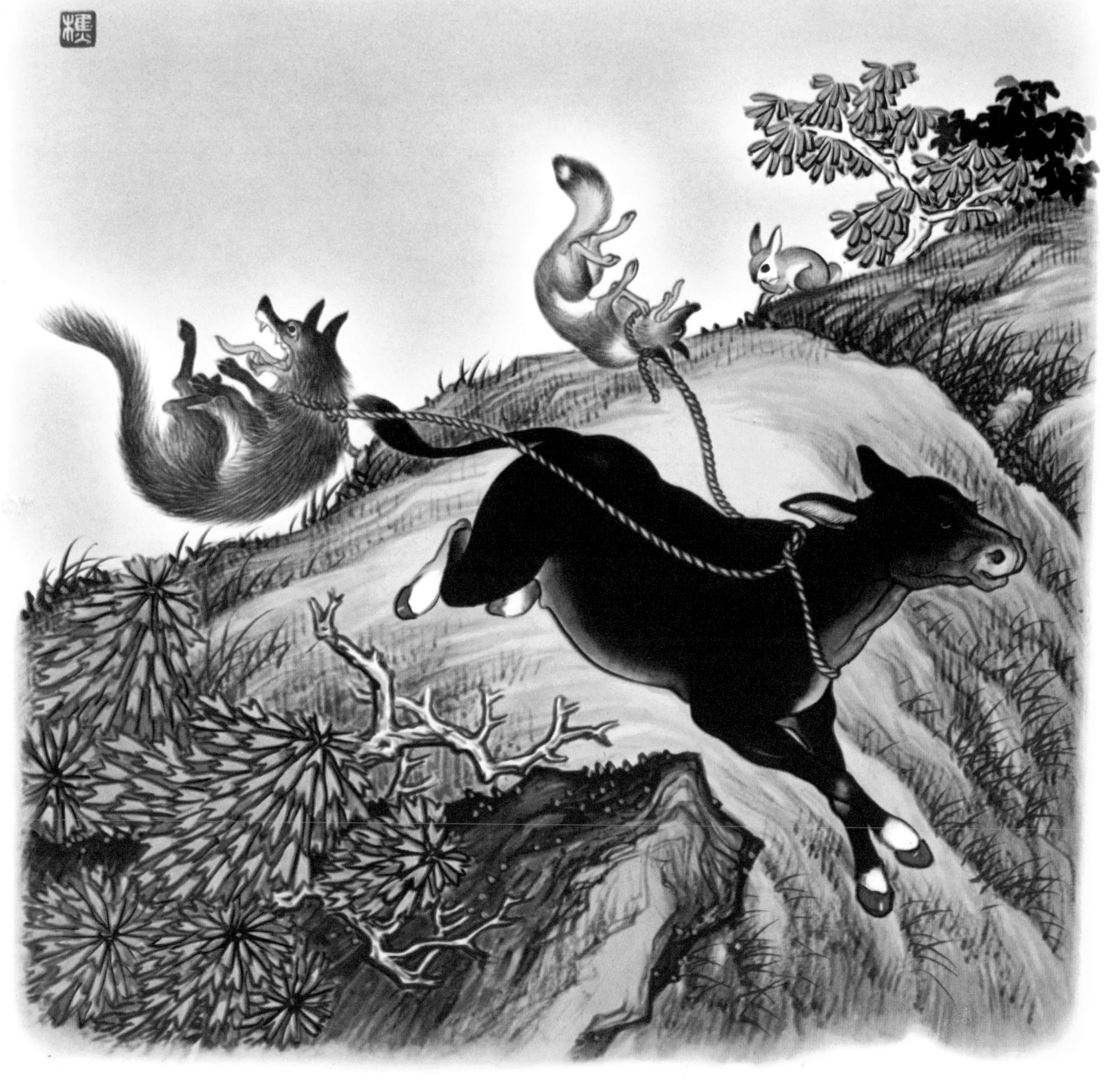

The Tower that Reached from Earth to Heaven

~ Tibet ~

FAR AWAY, on the western borders of Tibet, there is a country called the Land of Sekkim. In the Land of Sekkim there lives a race of men called Lepchas. In the race of men called Lepchas there was a farmer named Wu who had many little pigs.

One day, when the winds blew strong from the mountains of Tibet, Farmer Wu's little pigs all ran away. Now Farmer Wu loved his little pigs more than anything else in the world, so he wrapped a turban about his head and went

out to look for them. He climbed steep mountain passes and then he ran down into the valleys. For many days and many weeks he wandered on and on, always calling to his little lost pigs. He wandered so far that one day, to his great surprise, he found himself in Heaven.

Now, Farmer Wu had often wondered whether the country called Heaven was at all like the country called Sekkim, so great was his delight to see lovely rolling hills and many little pigs running about. He was just sure that some of them were his own pigs that had run away. He was so happy that he begged permission to stay there forever and ever. But the people in Heaven replied:

"Oh no, you are not yet ready to stay in Heaven. You must go back to Earth for a few years more."

The way seemed very long to Farmer Wu as he trudged back to Earth. But, when he reached the Land of Sekkim, he told the men called Lepchas all about the country called Heaven, with many little pigs running about. The men called Lepchas were so excited that they all decided they would build a tower to reach to Heaven.

"With a tower to reach to Heaven, we can climb into Heaven from our tower, without taking the long journey over the steep mountain passes."

Every man in the Land of Sekkim worked on the tower. One storey on top of another storey, up and up they built it, one storey atop another storey. As they worked on, they looked up and saw that they were getting nearer and nearer to Heaven.

As each storey was completed, they left one little man of Sekkim there to act as a guard.

So they worked on for many days and many months. Finally, after two long years, their tower needed only one more storey to touch the country called Heaven. Then the little men of Sekkim grew impatient.

"If only we had some big hooks, we could pull ourselves up into Heaven without building the last storey," they said to each other.

This was a fine idea. So the man at the top called out to the man on the storey below him: "Send us hooks!"

And he called to the man below him: "Send us hooks!"

And he, in turn, called out to the man below: "Send us hooks."

And *he* called to the man below: "Send us hooks!"

The Tower that Reached from Earth to Heaven

And so on, from storey to storey, the call made its way down to the Land of Sekkim. But on the way a very sad thing happened. The message was repeated so many, many times that it got twisted and, when it finally reached the bottom, instead of being still: "Send us hooks," it had become: "Cut us down!"

Whereupon the men called Lepchas got out their great stone axes and cut down the tower that reached almost to Heaven. It crashed in a heap on the ground.

And to this very day, far away on the western border of Tibet, there can be seen a flat green spot deep in a valley, right in the heart of a thick jungle forest. And the people say, as they pass that spot: "See that spot in the deep valley, that is the place where the Tower of Sekkim fell down, the Tower of Sekkim that almost reached the country called Heaven, where the hills are green and rolling, and many little pigs run about."

The Tower that Reached from Earth to Heaven

The Fox Outwits the Tiger

∾ West China ∾

ONE FINE day a tiger, in search of a tasty morsel for dinner, met a fine, plump fox, and was just about to sample him when the fox spoke up and said: "Come now, you don't really intend to eat ME!"

"Why not, pray tell?" demanded the tiger.

"Oh, there's a reason," answered the fox smugly.

"And what may the reason be, I should like to know?"

"Well, it's clear you don't know that Heaven has appointed me the ruler over

67

this district. You would scarcely dare to make a meal of an Officer of Heaven, I should think."

The tiger was taken aback. "Anyhow, I've got to have proof of that," he growled.

"Nothing more reasonable," agreed the clever fox. "Nothing simpler, either. Let us simply walk together through my domain, I in front and you behind me to see that I do not escape. Then you will see for yourself that all the beasts of the forest fear me as an Officer of Heaven."

So they started off down the road, the little fox walking along in front, his crafty eyes gleaming, and the tiger padding along close behind him.

As they came along through the forest, the animals paid no attention to Mr. Fox; but just as he had known would be the case, no sooner did they catch sight of their old enemy the tiger than they scurried off into the jungle as fast as their legs could carry them.

Then the sly little fox turned around to the tiger and said: "Now you see what happens when I make my rounds through my domain. All the animals fear the Officer of Heaven and run away."

"Well," answered the tiger, "since all the animals do seem to be afraid of you, it must be true, as you claim. You are truly an Officer of Heaven and of course I would not think of eating so important a person."

And the tiger turned about and started back into the forest himself. But suddenly he turned around again, bowed his head politely, and said: "Good-by, Your Excellency."

The Story of the Fairy Boat
∾ Central China ∾

ONCE upon a time there was a little boy whose name was Ho Lai. But little Ho Lai did not have a mother; he had only a cruel stepmother who was very horrid to him. Every day she sent him out with a basket on his arm to gather up frogs.

One day Ho Lai went out to the fields as usual, but while he was hunting frogs to appease his cruel stepmother, he came across a bag filled with coins. Not knowing to whom the money belonged, the boy decided to sit down and guard the bag, in hopes that the owner would return to claim it.

Nearly all day he sat there and watched. At last a man appeared, hunting for his lost money. He was so pleased to discover that Ho Lai had kept it for him that he offered the boy half the bag's contents. But little Ho Lai said that he did not wish for a reward, as he had done no more than his duty.

But it was now too late to catch frogs, and when the boy went home that evening with his basket quite empty, and his stepmother, on hearing his story, learned that he had refused an offer of money, she was so enraged that she promptly ordered him from the house. Giving him a basket and a stick, she drove him forth, crying that if he had no more sense than he had showed that day, he had best go beg for his living.

So little Ho Lai went out into the night. Fortunately, it happened to be the fifteenth of the eighth month, so the moon was full and golden and the night almost as bright as noon. As the boy walked aimlessly along, he kept his eyes fastened on the big friendly moon above. All of a sudden, he saw a tiny golden boat come floating down on a moonbeam. Tiny people were rowing the boat, others were dancing and singing, and still others played merrily on musical instruments.

Ho Lai thought he had never heard such lovely music, and he listened, entranced. Then, holding up his basket, he begged that the little boat might drop into it. To his great delight, the tiny boat did drop right into his basket, and the fairy people said that they had come to help him. Then the fairies went inside the boat, it shrank to a *very* small size, and Ho Lai placed it in his pocket. He wandered on until finally he came to the Emperor's palace, and there he got employment as a servant.

Now it happened that later on, by chance, the Emperor himself saw the tiny

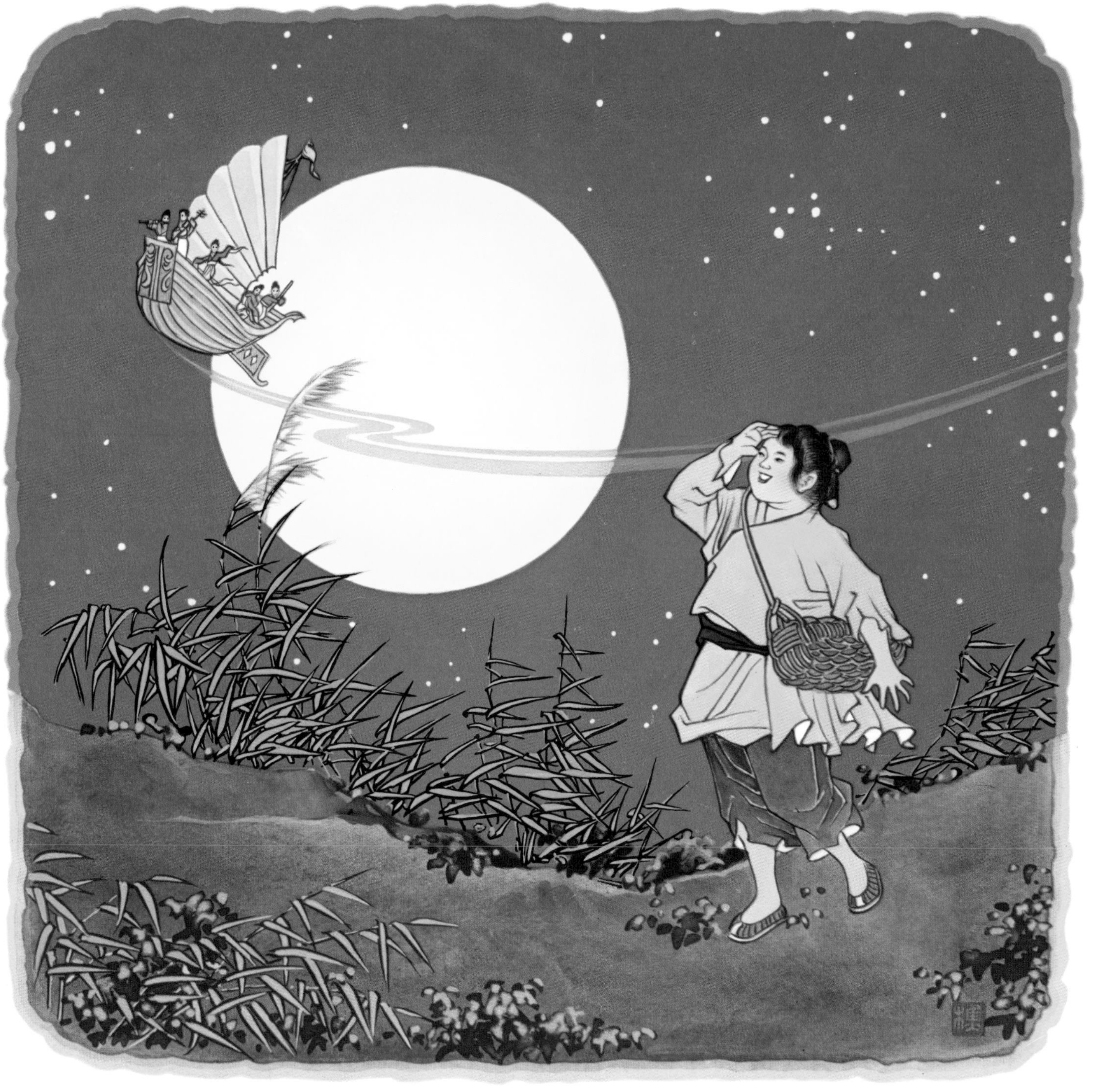

golden boat and heard the fairy music and he was so utterly captivated and charmed with it that he told Ho Lai he would give him his daughter in marriage, if only he could have the fairy boat. Ho Lai liked the princess, so he gave up the boat on the strength of this assurance. However, the Emperor, who was rather an undependable person, had no notion at all of carrying out his promise. That very night he issued orders that Ho Lai was to be placed in a haunted house.

This house was inhabited by two creatures, one with a red face, the other with a green face. It was their custom to eat up anyone who came there. Ho Lai was especially fortunate, however, for these two strange creatures unaccountably welcomed him as their friend, told him they would give their house to him, as they were rather tired of it; and then showed him where all sorts of treasures were concealed.

The Story of the Fairy Boat

The next day the Emperor, finding that Ho Lai was not only still alive, but was the possessor of much treasure, as well, repented of his evil designs, welcomed him as a son-in-law, and married him to the princess.

Then Ho Lai, with everything his heart could desire, thought of his father and his stepmother, still so poor. So he sent them a boatload of money with a message stating that he had lately married the Emperor's daughter so he could not come to see them, but was sending this money to help them along. Then he settled down with his princess and together they reared a dozen handsome children and they all lived happily together in a large and comfortable castle, with many conveniences. The Emperor, who became rather childish in his declining years, left more and more of the governing to his efficient son-in-law. The old Emperor preferred to sit in the garden on moonlight nights, playing with the golden boat and listening to the enchanted music of the fairy folk.

The Story of the Fairy Boat **73**

The Tiger in Court

~ *Southwest China* ~

ONCE upon a time there lived an old woman more than seventy years old, who had an only son. One day he went up to the hills and was eaten by a tiger. His mother was so overwhelmed with grief that she couldn't bear to live without him. She ran and told her story to the magistrate of the district, who laughed and asked her how she thought the law could be brought to bear on a tiger. But the old woman would not be comforted, and at length the magistrate lost his temper and bade her begone. She took no notice of what he said.

Then the magistrate, in compassion for her great age, promised her that he would have the tiger arrested. Even then she would not go until the warrant had actually been issued; so the magistrate, at a loss what to do, asked his attendants which of them would undertake the job of capturing the tiger and arresting him.

One attendant, Li Neng, who happened to be gloriously drunk, stepped forward and said that he would; so the warrant was immediately issued and the old woman went away to her home.

When Li Neng got sober, he was sorry for what he had promised; but since he thought the whole thing was probably a mere trick of his master's to get rid of the old woman, he did not trouble himself much about it. He went to the court and handed in the warrant as if the arrest had been made.

"Not so," cried the magistrate, "you said you could arrest the tiger, and now I shall not let you off."

Li Neng was at his wits' end, and begged that he might be allowed to ask the help of the hunters of the district. This was granted; so collecting together these men, he spent day and night among the hills in the hope of catching a tiger, and thus making a show of having fulfilled his duty. A month passed away, during which he received several hundred blows with the bamboo for not bringing in the tiger.

At length, in despair, he went to the Cheng-huang temple in the eastern suburb; he fell on his knees, and prayed for help. While he was kneeling in the temple a tiger walked in, and Li Neng, in a great fright, thought he was going to be eaten alive, but the tiger took no notice of anything, as he sat near the doorway.

Li Neng then cried out to the tiger: "O tiger, if thou didst slay that old woman's son, suffer me to bind thee with this cord." And, drawing a rope from his pocket, he threw it over the animal's neck. To his great surprise, the tiger, instead of pouncing on him, drooped his ears, allowed himself to be bound, and meekly followed Li Neng to the magistrate's office. The magistrate was alarmed to see a tiger standing before him, but he asked him: "Did you eat the old woman's son?" The tiger replied by nodding its head.

"That murderers should suffer death has ever been the law," announced the magistrate. "Besides, this old woman had but one son, and by killing him you took from her the sole support of her declining years. If however you will, from now on, be as a son to her, your crime shall be pardoned."

The tiger again nodded assent and accordingly the magistrate gave orders that he should be released. The old woman was very angry, thinking that the tiger ought to have paid with its life for killing her son.

Next morning, to her great surprise, when she opened the door of her cottage, there lay a dead deer. The old woman, by selling the flesh and skin, was able to purchase food. From that day on there was always something waiting for her. Sometimes the tiger would even bring her money and valuables, so that she became quite rich, and was much better cared for than she had been even when her own son was alive. She became very fond of the tiger, and she felt secure when he slept on the veranda. He often stayed near the house for a whole day at a time, and gave no cause of fear either to man or beast.

In a few years the old woman died. While the friends were assembled in the great hall of her new house, the tiger walked in and roared its lamentations, then walked quietly away. The next day while her relatives were standing round the grave, out rushed the tiger again, but this time the mourners, who did not know him, ran away in fear. But the tiger merely went up to the burial mound, and, after roaring like a clap of thunder, disappeared into the forest and was never seen again.

Then the people of that place built a shrine in honor of the Faithful Tiger, and it remains there to this day.

The Magic Pancakes at the
Footbridge Tavern

∾ *West China* ∾

IN A FAR-AWAY province in western China there was once, long ago, a famous inn by the side of the road. This inn was called the Footbridge Tavern. It was kept by a young woman who went by the name of Mrs. Number Three. No one knew a single thing about her, or even where she came from. She carefully guarded her real name as a great secret.

The inn was large, with many rooms, and these rooms were always filled with guests, because Mrs. Number Three always welcomed everyone to her

79

door. Even if they had no money, she would take them in without any charge. At the back of the inn she had built rows and rows of stalls for her many fine donkeys.

Now, one night quite late, a certain Mr. Chao stopped at this inn, and Mrs. Number Three gave him the room just next to her own. There were already six other guests stopping at the inn, and when Mr. Chao arrived, Mrs. Number Three was serving them all large goblets of wine. They all drank freely except Mr. Chao, who was not in the habit of drinking wine. All the guests chatted gaily together for a time, and then they all scattered to their rooms, and, in a short time, they were all fast asleep.

But Mr. Chao was restless and could not sleep. At midnight he heard some strange noises coming from the room of Mrs. Number Three. He peeked through a crack in the wall and saw the strangest sight he had ever seen in all his life. Mrs. Number Three had taken down from the shelf above her bed a wooden box. From this box she took out a row of tiny wooden figures. She set the wooden figures out on the carpet, then she blew on them, and, as if by magic, all the little figures came to life.

One little man scattered dirt on the rug. Tiny oxen drew a plough back and forth over the dirt. Then, from a sack, the little man scattered buckwheat seeds into the furrows. In less time than it takes to tell about it, little sprouts came up; the grain ripened and the little man set his mill to running and ground it into flour. He put the flour into a tiny sack and handed it to Mrs. Number Three.

Then the little man and the oxen lined up on the edge of the rug. Mrs. Number Three blew on them, exactly as she had done before. Instantly, the

The Magic Pancakes at the Footbridge Tavern

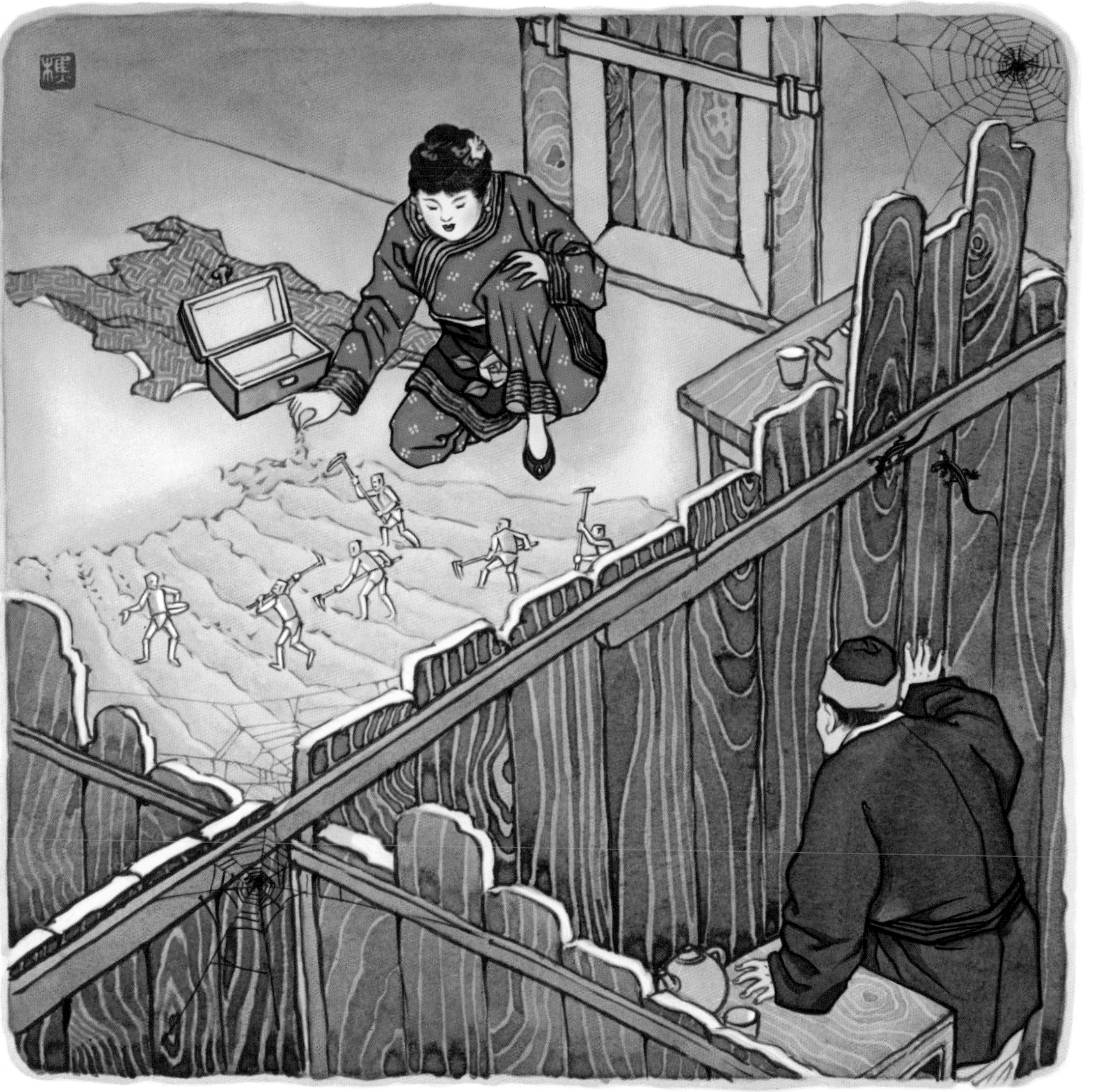

tiny creatures were changed back into wooden figures, which the lady stored away in the box. Then she covered the box and replaced it on the shelf over her bed.

Mr. Chao, who had watched all this with keen interest, knew that something quite special would happen the next morning. So he went down to breakfast very early. Already the six other guests were at table.

"Do sit down and have breakfast with us, Mr. Chao," called out Mrs. Number Three from the kitchen. "We are having delicious buckwheat cakes."

Just at that moment she came into the room, bearing a large platter piled high with steaming pancakes. She put three of the cakes on each guest's plate.

"I am sorry, I shall have to hurry away without stopping for breakfast," said Mr. Chao as he opened the door.

As he went out, he looked back over his shoulder and saw precisely the exciting thing he had been waiting for. As each guest bit into the magic buck-

The Magic Pancakes at the Footbridge Tavern

wheat cake, he dropped down on all fours and began braying like a donkey. In an instant they had all turned into donkeys. Mrs. Number Three laughed out loud as she cracked her long whip above their heads and drove them out to the donkey stalls behind the inn.

Several weeks later, Mr. Chao was passing along the same road. As he neared the Footbridge Tavern, he bought three buckwheat cakes from a traveling kitchen in the village, and carefully placed them in his pocket. Then he went up to the inn.

"Come in, come in, Mr. Chao," called out Mrs. Number Three, when she saw him. "You are just in time for breakfast."

"Thank you. I have traveled a long distance and shall enjoy your delicious buckwheat cakes this morning."

Mrs. Number Three piled cakes high on his plate and put three on her own plate.

At that moment a guest arrived at the front door and Mrs. Number Three left the table to welcome him.

This was just the opportunity Mr. Chao had been hoping for. He took from his pocket one of the pancakes he had bought in the village and exchanged it for one of the magic pancakes on his own plate. Then he quickly slipped that magic cake onto the plate of Mrs. Number Three.

"You are not eating your buckwheat cakes, Mr. Chao," scolded Mrs. Number Three as she sat down again at the table.

"I was waiting for you," he answered politely. "I am ready to eat now if you will eat with me."

"That seems quite fair," she said, sitting down at the table.

The Magic Pancakes at the Footbridge Tavern 83

The moment her teeth touched the magic pancake, she dropped down on all fours, braying, exactly as her former guests had done, and Mr. Chao promptly rode off on the back of the most beautiful gray donkey he had ever seen. She was so strong that he used her on all his travels.

One day he was passing a temple and the old priest was standing at the gate. He recognized the beautiful donkey as the former Mrs. Number Three, and he called to Mr. Chao to stop.

"I know that Mrs. Number Three played many tricks and made a lot of trouble," he said, "but now she has done penance long enough. Let us now break the magic spell that binds her to donkeyhood."

So the priest said a magic word, the donkey's skin dropped suddenly away, and there stood Mrs. Number Three before them. She laughed happily as she thanked the old priest for breaking the spell. Then off she went down the winding road.

She has never been heard of again from that day to this.

The Magic Pancakes at the Footbridge Tavern

The King of the Mountain
⏝ *North China* ⏝

IN THE far north of China there once lived, in a large cave on a mountain-side, a fierce tiger. This tiger was the terror of all the villages in the valley below. Every night he raided some herd of cattle, sheep, goats, or pigs, and he had even carried off several children. Not satisfied with taking just enough to eat, he seemed to delight in killing as much as he could.

All the people feared this King of the Mountain, as they called him. They did everything they could possibly think of to get rid of him, but all to no avail. Finally the officials offered a large reward to anyone who would follow the tiger to his cave on the mountain and kill him.

A large band of men went forth to kill the tiger, but although they waited at his cave for many days, they never even saw him. They decided at last that the beast must have another entrance to his lair; but though they hunted this secret entrance for many days, they were never able to find it.

Discouraged, they went to their great teacher, Lao Tzu, and told their troubles to him. He received them with great kindness and listened patiently to their story. When they had finished speaking, he told them that the root of the trouble lay in the fact that they did not really understand this King of the Mountain. As Lao Tzu was a friend to all the animals, he promised to see what he could do about the matter.

One day a little later, as the village people were busy with their work, a black cloud gathered over the valley and slowly settled over the village. As soon as

it touched the ground, it burst into a bright light. Then, to their surprise, Lao Tzu stepped from his cloud chariot.

"I have come to aid you," he said, "in the trouble you are having with the tiger who is King of the Mountain. Since no one among you really understands this old fellow, I shall have to go into the cave myself. Who will go with me?" he asked.

"I will go, I will go," each one shouted. Indeed, everyone was ready to go with Lao Tzu, but he said: "I cannot use all of you. Just one good strong man is enough."

So Lao Tzu looked about the crowd and selected a man named Wang. Wang was popular among the villagers, so they were glad to have him go.

"Now we shall need a torch and a nice little kid," said Lao Tzu. "Then we shall be ready to start off to the tiger's cave."

A farmer sent his son to fetch a kid from the field, and someone else brought

a torch. Wang carried the kid, Lao Tzu took the torch, and the whole company trailed along behind.

In a little while Lao Tzu turned around and told the crowd to return to their homes. "I must go alone with Wang to the tiger's cave," he said. So they all turned back to the village, talking and laughing about the queer method Lao Tzu was taking to catch a fierce tiger. "Of what use could a little kid and a torch be in such an affair?" they murmured.

When Lao Tzu and Wang arrived at the entrance to the tiger's cave, they walked boldly in. They had no need of the torch, for there was an opening in the top of the cave, and they could plainly see that the floor was covered with all kinds of bones from animals that the King of the Mountain had dragged back to his cave to devour. At one side they found a bed of sand on which the tiger slept. They placed the little kid on this sand bed and it curled up and was soon fast asleep.

"Now," whispered Lao Tzu, "we shall hide behind the rocks near the mouth of the cave and wait for the tiger to return."

"But I am afraid the tiger will kill our little kid," said Wang.

"Wait and see," replied Lao Tzu.

Thus they waited for several hours until the tiger returned to his home, carrying a freshly killed deer in his mouth. He slipped cautiously through the cave door and was just about to deposit the deer on the floor when he noticed the scent of another animal. Quickly he dropped the deer and, with a roar, began to sniff about. The tiger paced angrily to and fro, sniffing here and sniffing there; then, suddenly, to his astonishment, he saw not a fierce enemy but a little innocent kid sleeping on his bed.

At once his rage subsided, turning to love, and the tiger began to lick the kid like a cat licking its kitten. This awakened the little kid, which began to

play with the tiger, and the two rolled and tumbled on the floor like kittens. At last, when they became tired of play, they curled up together on the bed of sand and went to sleep.

The two men watched them until all was quiet, and then they, too, lay down behind the rock and went to sleep.

In the morning the tiger and the kid again played together in the cave until, suddenly, they made a dash for the door and were gone.

"Teacher! Teacher!" cried Wang to Lao Tzu. "Now the tiger is gone and we have not killed him!"

Lao Tzu replied: "Who said we were going to kill him?"

Lao Tzu and Wang followed the animals up on the hillside. There they saw the kid nibbling grass, and the tiger sitting by, watching him with loving eyes.

"While the tiger and the kid continue to live together, all will be well in the village," said Lao Tzu, and he turned to go.

"I will return in six months," he called to Wang as his cloud chariot came to the ground. He climbed into it and floated away.

Three months passed. One morning Wang decided to go again to the cave to see what was happening there. As he had done before, he hid behind a rock and waited for the tiger to return. When he came in sight, Wang saw that the kid was with him, as usual; but, to his great surprise, the tiger was greatly changed in appearance. His head was still that of a tiger, but his body was now that of a man. Wang watched while the tiger and the kid lay down on the sand together and went to sleep for the night.

Next morning, Wang walked back down the valley, wondering whether people would believe him if he told them what had happened. However, as

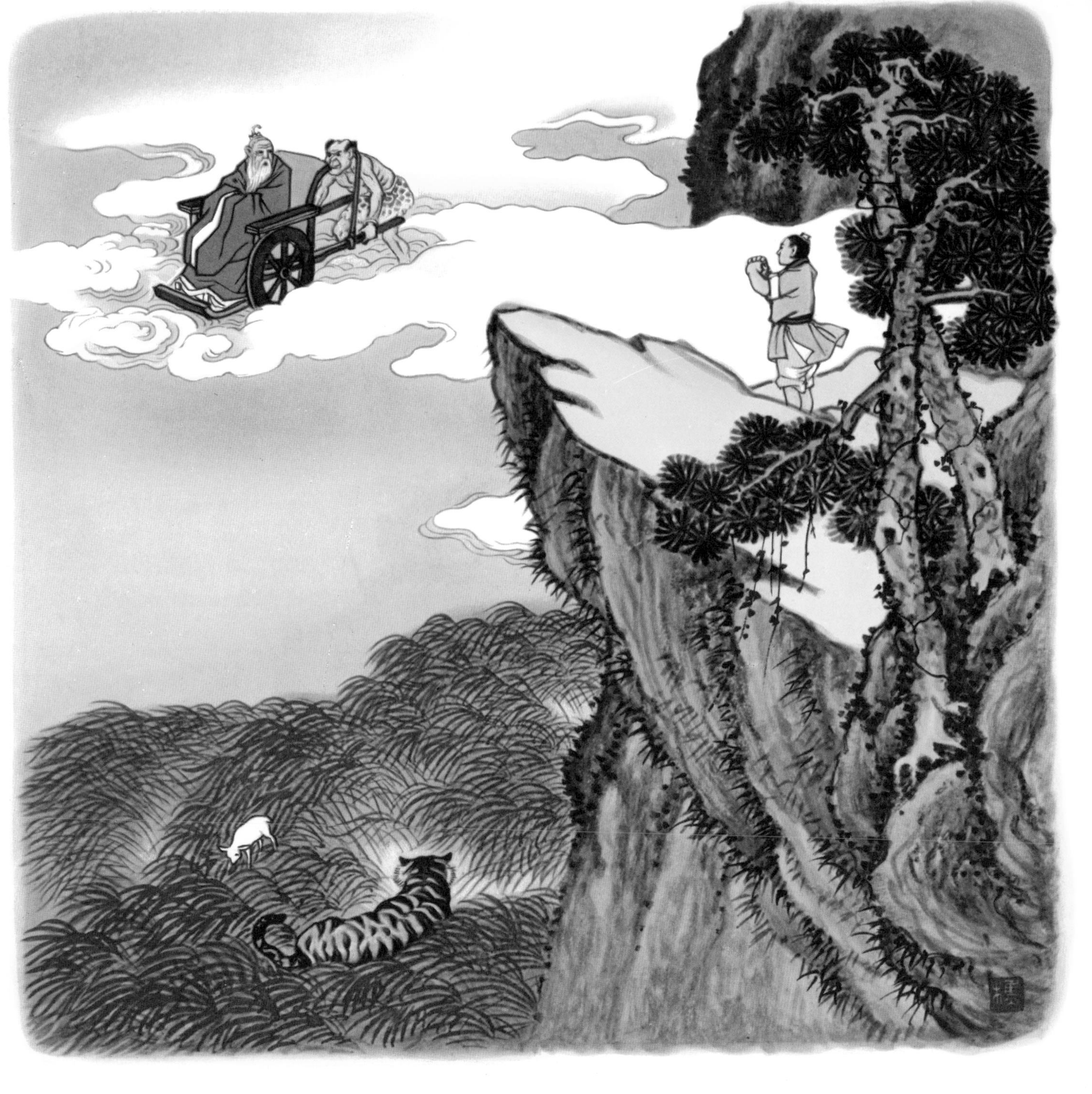

soon as he reached home, and before he could say a word himself, the villagers began to recount a strange tale of what had happened there the day before.

"A woman and her child were gathering firewood," they said, "when the mother heard a scream, and, turning around, she saw a great snake winding itself around her child. At that very moment a strange creature rushed out of the brush, killed the snake, and saved the child."

"She said the creature was half tiger and half man," they whispered.

When they had finished, Wang said: "The tiger's love for the little kid has transformed his nature. Even his body has become human."

Three more months passed. Everyone eagerly awaited the promised return of Lao Tzu. He could surely explain these strange events to them. One day his chariot was seen descending into the valley. When it touched the ground it burst into glorious brightness. Lao Tzu stepped forth and began to speak to the crowd.

"No more need you fear the King of the Mountain," said Lao Tzu. "For love has truly changed his whole nature. Not only is the tiger's nature changed, but each one of you is better because of the love that is working in your midst. Continue to be loving and your whole valley will be filled with peace."

As Lao Tzu ceased speaking, a young man approached the gathering. He came before Lao Tzu and bowed low. The villagers whispered: "The King of the Mountain! It is the King of the Mountain!" While they watched, Lao Tzu received the stranger into his glorious chariot, and together they floated away to the Western Heaven.

The Jackals and the Tiger

∾ Tibet ∾

ONCE upon a time there was a family of jackals, consisting of a father, a mother, and five young ones. After living for some time very comfortably near a large village, they found that the dogs of the village were becoming so numerous and so troublesome that they considered it necessary to change their place of abode. So one fine evening they started off and travelled away across the country, keeping a sharp lookout for some desirable spot in which they might settle down.

93

After a while they came to the edge of a forest, and having traveled for some little distance into the thickest part of the wood, they arrived all of a sudden at a tiger's den. The young jackals were a good deal frightened at the smell of the tiger's den, but Father Jackal reassured them, and said that he thoroughly understood tigers, and knew how to deal with them. So he went forward alone, and, peeping in, he found that the tiger was out, but that he had left a large quantity of deer's flesh, which he apparently had not had time to consume, lying in one corner.

So he called Mrs. Jackal and the children, and told them to go inside and have a good feed, and to make themselves quite comfortable.

After making a good meal himself from the deer's flesh, he said to Mrs. Jackal: "You and the children can now go to sleep; I shall go on to the roof of the den and keep a lookout for the tiger. When I see him coming, I shall rap on the roof, and you must at once wake up the children and make them begin to cry, and when I ask you what they are crying about, you must say that they are getting impatient for their supper."

Accordingly, Mr. Jackal went up on the roof, while his family settled down to sleep in the snuggest corner of the tiger's den. Shortly afterwards, Father Jackal heard a slight crackling among the dry leaves of the forest; and in the dim morning light he discerned the form of a great tiger approaching his den through the trees.

The Jackals and the Tiger

According to the arrangement he had made, he rapped with a loose stone upon the roof of the den, and Mrs. Jackal immediately woke up the young jackals and made them cry.

"What are those children crying about?" called out Father Jackal.

"They are very hungry, and getting impatient for their supper," was the reply.

"Tell them they won't have long to wait now," said Father Jackal, "the tiger will probably be home very soon, and we shall all be eating hot tiger's meat before long."

On hearing this the tiger was very much alarmed, and thought to himself: "What kind of strange animal can this be which has entered my den, and is waiting to cook and eat me on my return? It must certainly be a very fierce and terrible creature."

So, without waiting to investigate the matter any further, he turned tail and ran off as fast as he could through the forest. After running some distance, he came across an old baboon, with a great fringe of white hair all around his face. "Where are you running to, Uncle Tiger?" asked the baboon.

"Well," said the tiger, "the fact is, that a family of strange animals, who call themselves jackals, are at this moment in occupation of my den. As I was approaching my den, after a long night's hunting, one of the creatures was actually sitting on the roof, looking out for me, and as I got close up, I heard him tell his young ones that they were to have hot tiger's meat for supper. Fortu-

The Jackals and the Tiger

nately for me, he hadn't seen me, so I thought the best thing I could do was to make off as fast as I could, in order to avoid being eaten."

On hearing this the baboon was very much amused, and laughed heartily.

"Why," said he, "what a foolish tiger you are! Have you never heard of a jackal before? Don't you know that it is you who should eat the jackals, and not the jackals you? You come along with me, and I will soon show you how to deal with people like that."

The tiger was somewhat reassured on hearing what the baboon had to say, but even so, he was at first very reluctant to return again and to incur the danger of being eaten; but the baboon encouraged him, and finally they set off together, the baboon twisting his tail around the tiger's, in order to give him a feeling of support and confidence.

As they came nearer to the den, the tiger grew more and more timorous, and would advance only very slowly, ready to take flight at any moment. However, they went on together, tail-in-tail, until presently Father Jackal, on the

roof of the den, caught sight of the pair, and called out: "That is right, Brother Baboon, bring him along quickly; we are all half starved. But what do you mean by bringing only one of them? I had expected you would bring us at least two or three."

On hearing this, the tiger at once suspected that the baboon was in the jackal's employ, and that he was being led into a trap. Without a moment's hesitation, he turned about and fled into the depths of the forest. The unfortunate baboon, whose tail was tightly twisted round the tiger's, was unable to free himself, and was dragged and bumped hither and thither in the tiger's rush through the thickest and thorniest parts of the jungle. When at length the tiger paused, many miles away, to take breath, he looked back at his flanks, and all he saw of the baboon was a bit of its tail which had broken off and was still twisted around his own.

He never again returned to his den, which was occupied thenceforth by the jackals, who lived there for many years in peace and comfort.

The Jackals and the Tiger

The Fox Turns a Somersault

~ *South China* ~

THIS is the story of a poor countryman who lived all alone in a little mud brick house with a thatched roof. He was very poor and, since he had no wife, he cooked for himself only one meal each day. A kindly fox had been watching him through the window for a long time and she felt very sorry for him. So, one day, when he was out, she stole into the house and changed herself into a woman. She cleaned up the place, cooked a meal for him, and then disappeared.

This went on for some time, until the farmer determined to watch and find out who his kind and unknown visitor was. So he crouched behind a water jar and waited with his gun beside him. Before long he thought he saw the pointed nose of a fox and, sure enough, a sleek red fox slid through the hole in the wall into the room. He grabbed his gun and was just about to shoot the fox, when, to his amazement, she turned a somersault, and landed on her feet in the form of a beautiful woman. The fox skin fell to the floor.

The farmer waited for her to move into the next room. Then he crept out and took the skin and hid it under the pig trough.

At the end of the day, when the kindly woman's good deeds were all done, she searched everywhere for her fox skin so that she might go back to the forest, but she couldn't find it. Then she knew that she would have to remain a woman and would become the farmer's wife.

They lived happily together for many years, until, one day, the farmer said jokingly to one of his children: "Your mother is really a fox."

The little girls clung to their beautiful mother and cried out: "She is *not* a fox, she is our own darling mother."

His wife then demanded that he give the children proof of the terrible thing he had said, so he went over to the pig trough, and there was the fox skin just where he had hidden it.

He thought it would be a joke to show it to the children, but, as soon as his wife saw her old fox skin, she turned a somersault, slipped into the skin, ran out of the door into the forest, and they never saw her again.

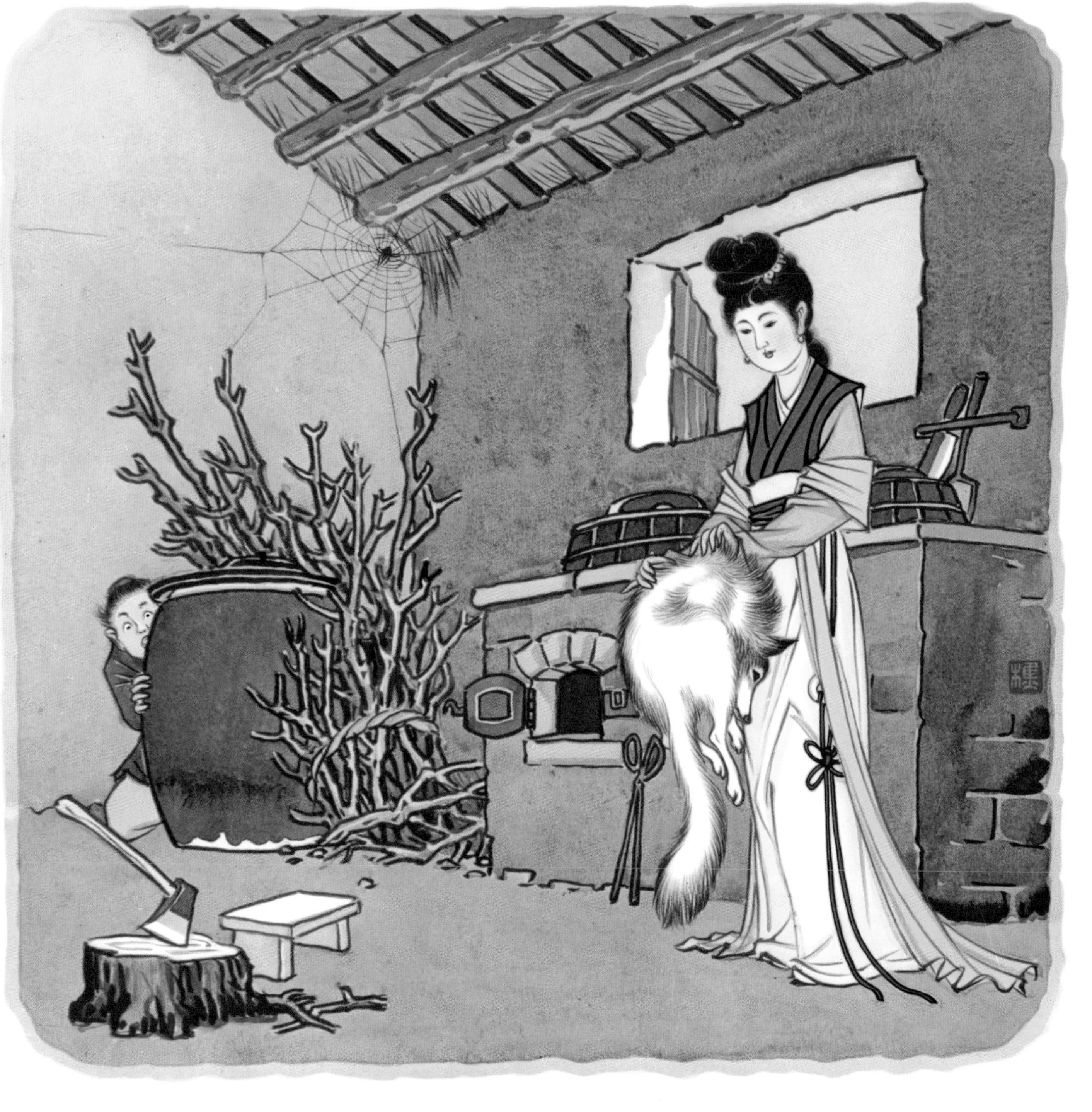

The Country of the Mice

~ *Tibet* ~

ONCE there was a king who ruled over a large country in which there lived a great number of mice. Generally these mice were very prosperous, with plenty to eat, but one year it happened that the country's crops were poor and the mice, who depended upon the spare grains left after harvest, found their stores running short before spring. The king of the mice, having determined upon a personal appeal to the king of the country, dressed up in his best gray suit and set off one morning to the king's palace. When the doorman announced to the king of the country that a mouse was asking to see him, His Majesty was greatly amused and ordered him admitted.

The mouse entered the audience chamber carrying a little silk thread which he presented to the king in place of the usual ceremonial scarf. "Good morning, Brother Mouse," said the king courteously. "What can I do for you?" The mouse bowed nicely and replied: "Oh King, as you know, this year our crops are short and we mice are threatened with famine unless we can borrow enough grain to see us through the winter. If you will loan us what we need, we will repay you with interest at the next harvest."

"Well," said the king, stroking his chin, "how much grain do you want?" Said the mouse: "We will require one of your big barns full." "How would you carry it away?" said the king. "Leave that to us," said the mouse. So the

king ordered a large granary to be thrown open to the mice with no interference whatsoever.

That night the king of the mice summoned all his subjects together and by the hundreds of thousands they invaded the barn. Each one picked up as much grain as he could carry in his mouth, on his back, and curled up in his tail; and when they were all through, the barn was empty and not a single grain of barley was left.

Next morning, when the king went out to look at his barn, he was astonished to find that the mice had been able to empty it so efficiently and he conceived a high opinion of their abilities. And when, at the following harvest, the king of the mice redeemed his promise by repaying the loan with interest, the king of the country was prepared to admit that the mice were trustworthy as well as clever.

Now it happened that shortly after this, the king of the country was forced to go to war with a neighboring kingdom that lay on the opposite shore of the river bordering the two countries. This other country was far richer and more powerful than the country where the mice lived, and its king soon assembled a huge army on the opposite bank of the river and began making preparations for invasion. The mice soon heard about this state of affairs and were distressed,

for they feared living under a strange and unsympathetic ruler. So once more the mouse king set out for the king's palace to offer the help of the mice. Despite his worries, the king was amused and asked how mice could help him when he couldn't even muster enough men to repel the enemy. "Leave it to us," replied the mouse; and the king, not knowing what else to do, agreed.

Next evening at dusk, the mouse king led several hundred thousand of his subjects to the river bank, where they found lined up a hundred thousand foot-long sticks which, at the mouse king's request, the king of the country had agreed to place there. The mice used these sticks as rafts to carry them across the river to the enemy camp, where the soldiers were all sound asleep. At a command from their king, the mice scattered over the camp and went to work, quietly doing as much destruction as possible. Some nibbled at the bowstrings

and slings of the soldiers' muskets; others gnawed the slow matches and fuses; still others bit off the clothes and pigtails of the sleeping men. In fact, they nibbled everything and left shreds and confusion in every direction. After a couple of hours' work, they reassembled at the river bank and re-embarked on their sticks, sailing noiselessly back to their own shore without having been detected by the enemy or having raised any alarm.

Next morning at daybreak a huge outcry arose from the enemy camp as each man, arising from sleep, found himself in sorry state—his clothes in tatters, his bow without a string, his rifle without a sling (and with no fuse or slow match to fire it), and no provisions for breakfast. As each accused the other of treachery, the whole camp was soon in an uproar. In the midst of the clamor, some shots were fired and bugles sounded on the opposite bank, and, thinking they were about to be overtaken, the whole army took to its heels. In a few minutes not a man was to be seen.

The king of the country of the mice was naturally elated at this easy victory, and quickly summoned the king of the mice to thank him for his good services. And, in accordance with a bargain made at the time the mice offered their assistance, he quickly set about to rid the country of the two things most harmful to mice—floods and cats. Since the burrows of the mice were in low land near the river, a small rise in the water always overflowed the level land and flooded their nests. The king of the country had a strong embankment built all along the river to ensure that water would, in future, be kept out. Cats are always, of course, persecutors of mice, and so the king banished them forever from the country, issuing an edict forbidding all persons henceforth, on pain of death, to keep cats of any kind. These rewards pleased the mice very much. The king of the country and the king of the mice each knew that the other was to be trusted and counted upon in all emergencies; and everyone lived together in that land very happily for the rest of their lives. Except cats.

The Country of the Mice

How the Deer Lost His Tail

∾ Southeast China ∾

ONCE upon a time, long ago, there were a little old woman and a little old man living together in a little old cottage at the edge of a big old forest.

Every day they walked together in their garden, for they loved to see the new buds opening to greet them, and the little shoots peeping up through the ground to surprise them. In the evenings they sat together watching the crackling logs in the grate. They were gentle people, happy and contented. But, as they chatted together, the little old woman often said: "We have our cottage

109

and our garden, and we are comfortable and happy here. But we do have one fear, alas. We do not fear the thunder, nor the lightning; we do not even fear the demons. But how we do fear the Leo. The Leo is certainly our great fear."

And she rocked back and forth. But the little old man could never find out what she meant by the Leo.

Outside their door, the night was so dark that it seemed to enfold the cottage with a dark mantle. It was the dark of the moon and the animals were prowling cautiously about through the forest. As the old couple talked together they did not know that a tiger lurked outside their cottage door; neither did they know that a thief was hiding nearby in the darkness.

Crouched at the door, the tiger was listening to what the old man and the old woman were saying. When he heard the old woman say that they had one great fear, of the terrible Leo, he put one ear right up against the crack of the door to try to hear more about this creature. The tiger had never known fear himself. After all, was he not the great King of the Forest? He was not afraid of the jackals, he was not afraid of the foxes, he was not even afraid of the lion. But he had never seen a Leo, and the thought of this unknown creature made him uneasy. Yes, the tiger began to feel afraid.

Now all this time the thief had been hiding in the darkness, waiting to steal the old man's cow. He began to creep nearer and nearer to the house when, all of a sudden, the thief spied something moving in the darkness. This was when the tiger crouched to put his ear to the crack of the door. The thief saw the outline of an animal and thought it must surely be the old man's cow, which he had long wanted to steal. So he crept closer and put his hand out to seize it; but, instead of finding a cow, his hand touched the tiger. The thief was so

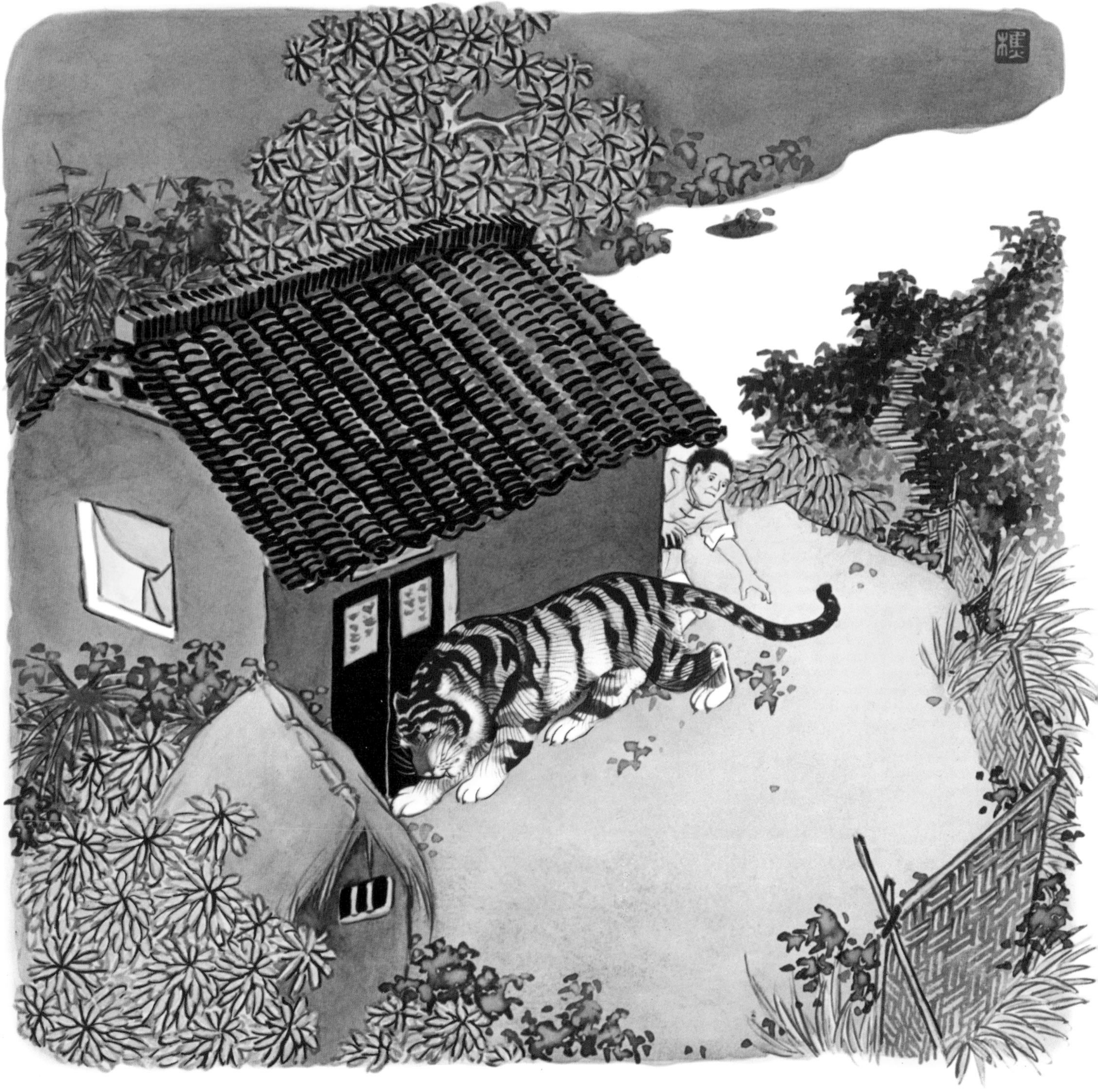

frightened that he scrambled as fast as he could in the dark to the cottage roof
to hide there from the tiger.

All this happened just as the tiger was listening at the cottage door and
wondering what he would do if he saw a terrible Leo. At that very moment,
through the denseness of the dark, he suddenly saw this strange figure scrambl-
ing to the roof, and the tiger thought to himself: "This must be the very Leo
that the old couple so greatly fear. Who will save me now?" He crept softly
around the house to try to escape from the fearful Leo.

Behind the house, at the edge of the forest, the frightened tiger met a deer.

He told the deer about the Leo, and how he had seen him climb to the cottage
roof. The deer was surprised and vastly relieved to find the fierce tiger so
gentle and friendly, but when he heard about the mysterious Leo, the poor
little deer trembled all over in a panic. "Alas, who will save me from the
terrible Leo?" he pleaded, with tears in his voice and in his big brown eyes.

Then the tiger pretended to be very fearless and wise. "Come with me, little deer, and I will take care of you; let us tie our tails together, so that we shall be able to help each other when we meet the Leo." The deer gladly consented, and he felt much safer after his tail had been tied to that of the strong tiger, so they crouched together close to the house. Just then, a tree branch broke off and fell with a loud crash. The thief, hiding on the roof, was so frightened that he leaped from the roof edge, landing almost on top of the deer. The poor little deer tried to escape into the forest, pulling his tail as hard as ever he could; but the tiger was pulling just as hard in the opposite direction.

Suddenly a dreadful thing happened! The little deer's tail broke right off!

The thief ran away. The tiger leaped into the forest in one direction, and the deer in another. But all that was left of the little deer's tail was a tiny tuft of fur. The rest of it was still tied in a knot at the end of the tiger's tail as he disappeared into the deep, dark woods.

And the dreadful Leo? No one ever saw *him*. The little old woman and the little old man put out the lamp and went off to bed and never knew all that had happened just outside their cottage door.

And this is exactly how the deer lost his tail.

The Little Hare's Clever Trick

∿ South China ∿

MANY, many years ago, the lion was appointed King of the Beasts. Every day all the other animals gathered together and bowed respectfully before him.

But one fine day the little hare fell sound asleep on a warm bed of hay. Finding it very comfortable, he got up very, very late and so he failed to appear with the other animals when they paid their homage to the King of the Beasts. When Master Hare arrived late, he crept in among the other animals, hoping to escape detection. But suddenly the mighty King arose, and his voice thundered

through the great hall: "You little rascal! You didn't come to pay respect to me, but stayed at home nibbling straw. It's hard to believe that you want to go on living!"

The frightened little hare thought quickly to himself: "Unless I can think of some clever story, the King of Beasts will surely kill me!" So he bowed low before the monarch and spoke with great respect: "O Mighty King, as I was on my way to do you homage, I passed by a little stream, and there, in a clear pool, I saw a little Demoness. I was terrified and tried to run away, but was able to escape only a few minutes ago."

At the thought of a Demoness, even the King of Beasts became alarmed.

"That Demoness," he asked anxiously, "did she harm you at all?"

"No," replied the clever hare, "she did me no harm, but she shouted at me and I was paralyzed by her voice. My heart felt as if it had been shattered into a hundred pieces."

"What did she say?" roared the lion.

"This is what she said, O King: 'You short-legged thing, where are you going and why do you run so fast?' I answered her: 'I am off to pay my respects to His Majesty, the Lion King.'

"Then she became very angry and shouted louder and louder: 'Well, at last we will clear up this matter! I have been trying for a long time to find this proud lion who calls himself a King. We shall see whether this lion is greater than I am! Go at once and tell him to come to this pool. We shall soon decide who is ruler among the animals of this forest!'

"O King, I do greatly fear for you," concluded the crafty hare. "But I will gladly carry your message back, if you have anything to say to her."

But the King of the Beasts made reply: "I have no message to give you. Lead me to her and I myself will say to her: 'O Demoness, let all know there is none on earth who can rule the animals better than I, their appointed King.' If she can overcome me, then, like a dog, I shall subject myself to her command."

Of course the little hare had not really seen a Demoness at all, so when the King decided to go himself to meet her, he was frightened anew. He thought to himself, his nose twitching: "How can I get out of this new plight I am in? I have an idea! I will lead him to a pool and then tell him that the Demoness is deep within the water. I myself will hide behind a bush and wait to see what happens when the lion sees his own shadow in the pool's clear waters."

When the Lion King arrived at the forest clearing where the hare led him,

The Little Hare's Clever Trick

he stalked proudly to the pool's edge and looked in to see the Demoness. In the reflection of the clear water he saw for the very first time his own fierce head. In his great shadow, each hair of his mane stood up, and his tail lashed furiously back and forth. Then the hare hopped out from behind the bush and shouted: "There she is, there she is!"

In great rage the Lion King roared aloud. Then he leaped into the water, grappling furiously with his own shadow. After the hare saw him sink to the bottom of the pool, he ran back into the forest to tell all the beasts that never again would they need to come together to pay their respects to the great Lion King.

The Little Hare's Clever Trick **119**